MOUNTAIN JUSTICE

Sissy Marlyn

Jury Pool

Justice

Sissy Marlyn

BEARHEAD PUBLISHING

- BhP -

Louisville, Kentucky

BEARHEAD PUBLISHING

- BhP -

Louisville, Kentucky
www.sissymarlyn.com
www.bearheadpublishing.com/sissy.html

Justice
by Sissy Marlyn

Copyright © 2008 Mary C. Drechsel
ALL RIGHTS RESERVED

Cover Design by Bearhead Publishing
First Printing - June 2008
ISBN: 978-0-9799153-5-2
1 **2** 3 4 5

Disclaimer

This book is a work of fiction. The characters, names, places, and incidents are used fictitiously and are a product of the author's imagination. Any resemblance of actual persons, living or dead is entirely coincidental.

NO PART OF THIS BOOK MAY BE REPRODUCED
IN ANY FORM, BY PHOTOCOPYING OR BY ANY
ELECTRONIC OR MECHANICAL MEANS,
INCLUDING INFORMATION STORAGE OR
RETRIEVAL SYSTEMS, WITHOUT PERMISSION
IN WRITING FROM THE COPYRIGHT OWNER/AUTHOR

Proudly Printed in the United States of America.

Acknowledgements

Thanks to the following great people, places, or things that helped to add flavor, description, and life to *Justice*:

Little Pigeon River – A familiar waterway running throughout Gatlinburg, Tennessee

Gatlinburg, Tennessee – An awesome mountain town I've enjoyed visiting many times

The Hemp Store – One of many stores in Gatlinburg

Bowie knives – A popular brand of knives

Fairfield Inn – Great brand from the Marriott chain of hotels

Morton's Antiques – A charming antique store in Gatlinburg, TN

LMPD – Police department in Louisville, KY

Roscoe and Enos – Two loved, comical characters from the Dukes of Hazard series

Hendersonville, Tennessee – A cozy little community near Nashville

Hendersonville Police Department – The police department in Hendersonville, TN

Nashville, Tennessee – Fantastic place to visit or live

Jimmy Durante – an American singer, pianist, comedian and actor, whose distinctive gravel delivery, comic language butchery, jazz-influenced songs, and large nose helped make him one of America's most familiar and popular personalities of the 1920s through the 1970s

The Eagles – An awesome rock and roll/country band like no other

Lone Ranger – A long-running, old-time radio and early television show created by George W. Trendle and developed by writer Fran Striker

anywho.com – A great resource for locating phone numbers
Wal-Mart – Popular department store that I shop at a lot
ABC – Popular network I like to watch
I Will Remember You – Popular, hit song by Sarah McLachlin
Beverly Gardens Park – Park in Beverly Hills, California
Pigeon Forge Police Department – The police department in Pigeon Forge, TN
Gatlinburg Police Department – The police department in Gatlinburg, TN
Sevier County Jail – Jail in Sevierville, TN
Dolly Parton – Delightful and famous country singer/actor
Petrus – Nightclub in downtown Louisville, KY
George Forman Grill – A great gadget for cooking, delicious, quick meals
Fort Sanders Sevier Medical Center – 79 Bed Acute Care Hospital in Sevier County
IPOD – Delightful devise for listening to modern music
Doritos – Savory, crunchy snack from Frito-Lay
Fort Sanders Sevier Nursing Home – A skilled care facility in Sevier County
Dateline – a popular nighttime television series
Oprah – a popular daytime series

Other Novels Written by *Sissy Marlyn*:

Intimacies
Illusions
Indecisions
(The "I" Women's Fiction Series)

Bardstown
Bowling Green
(The "B" Women's Fiction Series)

(The third, and final, *Bluegrass*, coming soon!)

Jury Pool – Summons to Die
Jury Pool – A Killer's Mind
(The first two Mystery novels in the *Jury Pool* Series)

For more information and synopsis of each novel, check:

www.sissymarlyn.com

www.bearheadpublishing/sissy.html

Dedication

*To my continually growing fan base,
Keep reading, and I'll keep writing!*

*To my Bearhead,
Thanks so much for your love and support!*

*To my sisters,
Whose sharp 'old' eyes help me proof these novels.
Let's see if you read the Dedication Page.
Hee hee!*

Prologue

The West Prong of the Little Pigeon River surged along the riverbed in Gatlinburg, Tennessee. Ample, multi-shaped, scattered rocks momentarily splintered the watercourse up and down the river. But the persistent, vibrant stream leapt and flowed over, and around, each stone obstacle and continued its forward haste, lapping and dancing alongside the densely wooded banks under the cover of darkness.

Early morning – three a.m. – the rush of the river, foraging animals, and chirping birds were primarily the only sounds stirring the otherwise serene environment. Sporadically, a stray car would also disturb the quiet, snaking its way along the Parkway and leaving a trail of exhaust as it passed the many shops, hotels, sites of amusement, and eateries in town. But this particular morning, a commotion of a different, sordid kind was about to transpire in this hushed mountain town.

Actor Jameson Thornton, whose claim to fame came from one hit television show and several blockbuster movies, stood on a stone ledge behind The Hemp Store overlooking the Little Pigeon River. A motion activated security light, hanging high on the back of the building, lit Jameson's stocky form and the concrete protrusion under his feet. This light also illuminated the other man facing Jameson, and more importantly, the raised gun in this individual's gloved hand.

Even though the area where these two men were standing was lighted, it was still fully obscured from view from the street or the sidewalk – not that anyone was walking on the sidewalk at this early hour in November. Jameson dared to speak up, the cold air causing smoke to roll out of his mouth with each word, "Look, I've done what you've asked and willingly come to this spot. Now, what do you want from me? I don't have a lot of cash in my wallet, but you can have what I've got. You can also have my gold watch," Jameson offered. He rolled back the sleeves of his winter Izod jacket and silk shirt to point to the fancy Rolex on his wrist. The gold gears and casing shimmered in the light.

The fearful tremor in Jameson's voice amused, and pleased, his captor. "What do I want from you?" Jameson's keeper repeated, smiling. "Let's see…" Pausing, snickering, and tapping a gloved index finger to his lips, the brandisher of the gun continued, "Let's start with you putting these on your wrists." With that statement, this man reached in his back pocket and pulled forth a pair of handcuffs. Giving them a slight toss, they landed with a clatter close to Jameson's feet.

"Handcuffs?" Jameson questioned, his brow furrowing. He stooped to pick them up, keeping his eye on the pointed gun at all times. "Why do you want me to put these on?"

"You sure do ask lots of questions, don't you?" the scoundrel asked, sounding perturbed. "Surely you don't question your directors like this when you're filming a movie or television show," the villain stated; then cackled and spurted, "By golly, that's it! I want you to think of me as your director. I'll tell you exactly what I want from you, and you just follow my instructions. Have you got that?"

"Even a director will tell you *why* they want you to do something," Jameson disputed, dangling the handcuffs from one hand.

"I'm sure that's correct," the rogue agreed. "So I'll tell you exactly *why* you need to do as I say and shut your big yap." The man took a step closer to Jameson, and he aimed the gun straight at his face. "If you don't do what I ask of you and you keep on yapping, I will blow your fucking head off. Now, how's that for instruction? Do we understand each other? Put your hands behind your back and snap on those damn handcuffs. Got it?"

"Okay! Okay!" Jameson agreed, his eyes growing large as he heard the bullet chamber. Raising his empty hand, Jameson established, "I'll put the handcuffs on. Just don't do anything rash."

"Oh, I would never do that," his assailant assured him, his teeth showing as his lips spread apart. The thug's insides also quivered. Excitement such as this had not been experienced by this individual in a long while. *The thrill from this kill will be that much sweeter*, the gunman pondered, knowing he had planned this execution with an agenda in mind. Hearing the handcuffs snap closed, this abominable creature issued another order, "Turn around and kneel down."

"Look, you know who I am. I'm a movie star. I've won Oscars for some of the movies I've been in. So you know I'm bound to have lots of money," Jameson reminded the wrongdoer. Sweat trickled down the back of his neck and beaded on his forehead, even though it was a chilly morning. "I could make you rich in the blink of an eye," Jameson said, snapping his fingers. He hurried on, "Just a few phone calls are all it would take. So why don't you just take my wallet and my watch for now? Then we can go to my chalet, and I'll make some calls and get you tons more money. You have everything to gain by letting me live. Hurting me won't gain you anything."

Oh, how I love to hear them plead and negotiate. Isn't bargaining one of the stages of death? And the fear in his eyes! the beast savored.

The brute lowered his gun. "You know you have a point," he agreed. "But I can't take you back through town with those handcuffs on. I've got the key in my inside jacket pocket. I wasn't going to hurt you anyway. I was just going to rob you and leave you here handcuffed. I figured that would scare you and then you might stay put for awhile while I got away. But I like the idea of you getting me more money even better. Turn around and I'll unlock those handcuffs. Then we'll go to your chalet and execute your financial plan for my future of luxury."

"Now you're talking," Jameson agreed. He slowly turned, looking back over his shoulder at the ruffian.

"Hold your hands out from your back," his captor instructed.

Jameson did as asked, pushing his arms out as far as he could get them. He was not going to give this individual another chance at hurting him – at least not without a struggle. When his hands were released, Jameson fully intended to wrestle the gun away from this scumbag. Even though Jameson no longer worked out on a daily basis, as he had in his younger days – he was fifty now – Jameson believed he was still fit enough to give his smaller foe a decent run for the money.

As the degenerate drew close to Jameson's hands, Jameson watched out of the corner of his eye, awaiting his freedom and mentally preparing his counter-offensive. Jameson fleetingly relished the fantasy of securing the gun and then discharging it, killing this troublemaker once and for all – *after all, wouldn't that just be fitting? Mountain justice I think they call it!*

Jameson glimpsed his nemesis's hand reaching inside his jacket. The welcomed thoughts – *It won't be long now and I'll be free. And then this dirt bag will get what he deserves* – had no more than registered in Jameson's mind than his assailant's hand whipped out of his jacket.

In the blink of an eye, Jameson's lower back – the space below the ribs and above the hip bone – transformed from skin, muscle and organs into the Grand Canyon. A razor-sharp Bowie knife obliterated protective tissue and muscle and more importantly, Jameson's kidneys. Shock instantly immobilized Jameson's body. He could not even open his mouth to shout. Red Niagara Falls simultaneously plummeted from his mortal wound. Urine and feces defiled the ground around Jameson's feet and turned pleasurable mountain smells into a formidable stench.

Seconds later, Jameson's legs became a closing accordion and he crumpled facedown on the concrete pad, plopping in the gathering pool of blood, urine and feces. Struggling to draw one final breath, a single bubble formed in his blood. Famed actor Jameson Thornton ceased to be.

Chapter 1

In the Thick of Things

At eight-thirty a.m., Ann Dryden and Camille Scofield, two middle-aged, female tourists, ventured from the Fairfield Inn just inside Gatlinburg. They crossed the street, listening with amusement to computer generated sounds – cannon blasts and cartoon characters talking – coming from the miniature golf course beside their hotel. They walked past several rental offices and a tattoo parlor, feeling carefree and trying to ignore the chill in the air.

Since it was November, the temperature was in the low thirties and the wind chill was lower than that. Parka jackets, gloves and warm headgear – hoods on coats and earmuffs – warded off the cold and helped these ladies enjoy their casual time outdoors in the mountains.

Their brisk morning stroll carried them along the sidewalk that ran beside the Little Pigeon River. Clouds of breath could be seen as they chitchatted, laughed, and traipsed this path – athletic shoes striking pavement. As they walked, they derived pleasure and tranquility from the frosted mountains towering all around them. The splashing, fluttering Little Pigeon River added even more harmony to their trek, and the prevalent aroma of smoldering firewood warmed their insides as they envisioned balmy flames leaping in private residences and hotel fireplaces along their path.

As Morton's Antiques came into their sightline, Camille's unshielded, sharp blue eyes noticed some strange reddish-brown matter on the sidewalk in front of the store. *Wonder what that is?* She silently pondered. *Did someone spill some paint or stain?*

Ann had not noticed the discolored pavement yet, because she was looking off to the right at the Little Pigeon River. She stopped with a start and removed her sunglasses when her eyes caught sight of the old, dilapidated footbridge running across the river beside the antique store. Something was hanging between one of the rotted opened section of the bridge, and that *something* appeared to be a man.

"Wh...what's that?" Ann's shaky voice asked her friend, pointing toward the bridge.

Noting Ann had stopped and following her gaze, Camille diverted her eyes, and her attention, from the soiled sidewalk to the bridge. When she saw what her friend was pointing at, she gasped. "My God! That can't really be a body, can it?" Then she pointed out, "That looks like blood on the concrete leading over to the bridge too."

"Could it be a prank that some kids pulled at Halloween, and no one's taken it down yet?" Ann theorized, not wanting to believe that there could actually be a dead body along their path.

It was early November, only a week past Halloween, and she and Camille had visited Gatlinburg at Halloween several years ago. They discovered that the kids did get into plenty of mischief and pranks here. There had been tons of silly string all over the sidewalk and merchant windows down through town.

"Well, there's only one way to find out whether it's a prank or not. Let's take a closer look," Camille suggested.

Ann was ambivalent to follow her friend's suggestion, and as Camille started forward again, she crept behind her at a snail's pace. As Camille slinked up to the gate leading onto the bridge, she reached out to place her gloved hands on top to lean forward to get the best possible look at the *thing* dangling from the bridge. But before Camille's hands could land, a sharp male voice rang out, "Don't touch that gate!" Startled, both women's bodies shuddered. They turned to find a tall, slim, dark-haired man, in a red winter jacket, jeans and loafers, charging toward them and pointing with ungloved hands toward the gate. They both froze in place, fearful and unsure.

"Sorry to scare you, ladies," he said, dropping his hands to his sides. Smoky vapor escaped his mouth as he rushed on, "But you need to understand that you are standing in a crime scene. I need you both to keep your hands to yourself and not touch anything. You also need to be careful where you walk. I need for the two of you to get back on the sidewalk over there," this stranger told them, raising a hand again to jab a finger in the direction from whence they had come. "I've already called the police. I need for you both to go back over there. Or cross the street."

Camille's curiosity got the best of her and she turned her head to look back at the bridge. When she did, her eyes captured a decent glimpse of the 'thing' hanging from the bridge. She noted what looked like black hair and fingers being moved back and forth by the water. As her eyes traveled upwards, the grotesque, open, organ-exposing gash and the blood saturated tatters hanging on the man's back came clearly into view. A light bulb came on bright for Camille; she gagged, struggled for breath, shivered, and spun around. With large panicked eyes and a trembling hand, Camille grasped Ann's arm and stated, "We need to do what he says."

"Please do," Scott pleaded, pointing to the sidewalk again. "The police should be here shortly."

As Camille and Ann vacated the parking pad beside Morton's and retreated several paces along the sidewalk,

Camille sank her gloved hands deep into the pocket of her down-filled, mid-length winter coat. Her entire body was suddenly quivering inside and out. All she wanted to do was turn around and go back to the hotel, pack, and get out of town. But Camille realized they could not leave before the police got there. Fleeing the scene of a crime could make them look guilty. She could not believe this awful thing had happened in the peaceful town of Gatlinburg, one of her favorite places to visit. She struggled not to burst into tears.

A moment later, the insistent, disquieting wails, of police sirens hammered away at all their eardrums. A few seconds after that, three Impalas, plainly marked as Gatlinburg police cruisers, crossed lanes to skid to a halt, facing the wrong direction, in front of Morton's Antiques and the adjacent merchant, The Hemp Store. The cars' sirens were silenced but their flashing lights were left on.

A uniformed officer leapt from each vehicle. They all converged upon the sidewalk, not mindful of the blood trail their scuffling feet might be disrupting. Very few homicides occurred in Gatlinburg.

Before the policemen had gotten very far, the same dark-haired stranger, who had ushered the ladies out of the crime site, leapt out in front of them. He shouted at the officers, looking like a mad man with his arms flailing and his fingers pointing, "Watch where you are stepping! You may be destroying evidence."

The policemen all stopped their forward gait. Stepping sideways, they hugged the curb. Narrowly escaping rubbing their bodies against their police cruisers, they cautiously – hand near guns – approached the shouting, unidentified, wild man.

"Let's start by ya identifyin' yerself and yer business here," the first policemen to approach demanded. This officer's large sinewy arms looked as if they could easily fold the stranger's body into a pretzel.

"My name is Scott Arnold, and I'm the person that called you guys when I discovered this body this morning," he wasted no time sharing. "You are all standing in the middle of a crime scene, and your feet and hands can easily contaminate it. Do you have any police tape in your cars? We need to cordon off the sidewalk from the parking area beside The Hemp Store to this parking area in front of that bridge," Scott instructed them.

"How is that ya know so much about police procedure?" One of the other officers questioned, a cynical scowl on his small, pinched face.

"I was a crime scene investigator in Louisville, KY a few years back. You need to call in your investigative team. But first, we need to secure the crime scene. Those ladies over there are tourists," he informed them pausing and pointing. Hurrying on, Scott justified his urgency to secure the crime area, "Those ladies were just out for a morning stroll, and they almost contaminated the scene. You've heard the term curiosity killed the cat… Well, this time it will be curiosity killed the crime scene," he pointed out. Taking a quick breath, Scott rambled on, "I'm sure as it gets later, there will be many more people out and about. We don't want them all traipsing through the crime scene…possibly destroying evidence…like you, and these ladies, almost did," he freely accused.

"Jest what we need…a wise guy," the third officer grumbled under his breath, rolling his eyes and stroking his beard. A deep, disapproving scowl played between his mustache and whiskers.

"Call me whatever you like," Scott conceded, shrugging. But he dared to continue, "All I know is you guys are the ones that started barging through a trail of blood, and we don't know what your footsteps, or the imprints of your shoes, might have destroyed. A mistake like that can be the difference between getting a conviction in a crime and allowing a killer to go free." Scott drove his crucial point home.

"Yeah...well...ya're standin'" in *our* crime scene right now," the policeman Scott had chastised reminded him. "So why don't ya just go on over yonder with the ladies..." he strongly suggested, waving a finger. "And let us secure *our* crime site?"

"I'd be more than happy to," Scott agreed, turning and walking the few paces over to the women. "Ladies," he addressed, giving them a nod. He sank his hands far into the pockets of his jacket.

Ann nodded back at Scott. Camille, however, was looking down at her shuffling feet, seemingly ignoring the man who had joined them. Not having sunglasses to shield her eyes, they had been pained by the unrelenting strobe of the squad cars' iridescent lights, and since she did not wish to look the other direction toward the body, she stared at her feet and the pavement around them now. Camille just wished, more than anything, that she and Ann could leave.

As if reading her thoughts, Camille heard Ann ask Scott, "I guess the police need for us to stay put, huh?" Since Ann had heard most of what Scott had said to the officers, she considered him to be an authority figure now.

"Yeah," Scott replied. "But hopefully, you won't have to wait too much longer. That is if Roscoe, Enos and Enos Wannabe can get their acts together over there," Scott stated with distaste, grimacing as he watched the three officers begin to work together to string yellow tape around the crime scene area as he had indicated.

Ann hoped that Scott was correct, and they did not have to stay here much longer. She just wanted to turn around and go back to the hotel. Her continental breakfast tossed in her stomach as she found herself glancing over at the body on the bridge for the umpteenth time.

Ten more minutes passed – seeming like an eternity to the ladies – before an unmarked car pulled up and parked behind the three police cruisers. A chunky man with thinning brown hair, dressed in a black, insulated, unzipped, winter jacket, slacks, dress shirt and tie, climbed out of the driver's side of the car. He slipped on a pair of latex gloves. A younger, more fit, man, also in a winter jacket and dress clothes, opened the passenger door and stepped out. This man's gloved hands held a camera.

"Ah...at last, their crime scene investigative team," Scott surmised.

Both Camille and Ann were happy to hear this statement. They hoped their time here would be short now. As much as Camille tried to ignore it, when the wind blew a certain direction, she could swear she smelled the rancid odor of butchered meat.

Scott saw one of the uniformed officers speak to the driver of the unmarked car. He watched as the officer pointed to him and the ladies. Then Scott saw the detective look over at him and the women and slowly approach. This man walked very close to the curb, circumspectly trying to avoid disrupting any evidence that might be found on the sidewalk. *At last, someone who knows what they are doing*, Scott contemplated as he watched the detective approach.

"Hi, I'm Lieutenant Carter Jetro," he introduced himself. "Which one of ya'll made the initial call about the body?"

"Lieutenant, I'm Scott Arnold. I discovered the body," Scott spoke up, offering his hand.

The plastic tips of the lieutenant's glove made brief contact with Scott's hand before, on a mission, Carter persisted, "How'd ya come upon the body, Mr. Arnold?"

Scott's chocolate eyes locked with the lieutenant's no-nonsense, coal brown eyes and he replied, "I was driving up the Parkway when I spied the body hanging from the bridge. Then I spotted what looked like a blood trail in front of Morton's and The Hemp Store. So I pulled my van into the parking area beside The Hemp Store. When I got out of my van to investigate, I noted that the blood trail grew denser the closer you got to the concrete pad in back of The Hemp Store. I discovered that the majority of blood, as well as some bodily waste, are on the ground in back of The Hemp Store. From this, I conclude that the murder occurred in back of The Hemp Store, a logical place, since it is out of sight of pedestrians and traffic. Then the killer drug the body over to the bridge, cut the lock on the gate, and hung the body there to drip dry…so to speak."

"You seem very methodical in your investigation of this crime…and also very detached emotionally…" Carter noted, his mouth a tight line.

"As I told your officer buddies, I was a crime scene investigator in Louisville, Kentucky a few years back. I guess investigating crimes is like riding a bike…you never forget how."

"Do ya still live in Louisvill', Mr. Arnold," the lieutenant inquired.

"No sir. I live in Hendersonville, Tennessee now, with my wife of a few months," he told him.

"So what brought ya into Gatlinburg so early this mornin'?" Carter interrogated.

Scott shifted from one foot to the other and glanced down at the ground before he looked back into Lt. Jetro's daunting eyes and answered, "I'm a private eye and I was hired for a case in this area. I just happened upon the crime scene."

"What a thing to just *happen* upon," the lieutenant grumbled, an edge of mistrust in his voice. His intrusive, haunting eyes, so dark that it almost appeared his pupils were dilated, bore holes through Scott. His mouth was a pinched line.

Before Scott could reply to Lt. Jetro's question, Camille put her two cents in, stating, "We were just out walking and *happened* upon the body too. We thought it was a Halloween prank. I had no idea it was a real body until this man..." she said, pointing to Scott. She took a breath and rushed on, "This man stopped us from touching the gate when we went to take a closer look because he said we were in the middle of a crime scene. Then when I...I...well...when I did take a good look...." she broke eye contact with the investigator and her body shook. "Who would do such a horrible thing?"

Ann put her arm around her shorter friend to comfort her. She was glad she had not gotten to take a *close* look at the body. The few glimpses she had gotten had made her skin crawl and her insides dance like Jell-O.

"Okay," Carter said, feeling sorry for the ladies' distress. "I'm goin' ta have officer Riley here ta gather some contact informat'n from y'all in case we have any further questions. Thanks for hangin' around and givin' your input. And thank you, Mr. Arnold for helpin' us to secure our crime scene. If y'all excuse me, I need ta began processin' evidence."

"Go to it," Scott replied. The ladies merely shook their heads in agreement.

As Lt. Jetro had indicated, a uniformed officer, with a shiny silver name badge with *Riley* on it, stepped forward. The ladies both pulled a driver's license from a jean pocket, and the policeman recorded their information on a small, handheld pad and simply wrote *tourists from Clarksville, Indiana* by their names. Once the policeman had recorded the women's information, Camille asked him if they were free to go. He said that they were, so the ladies turned and scurried away, headed back to their hotel, and no doubt home to Clarksville after that.

Scott had fished his wallet out of his back pocket and had his license pulled forth. He handed his ID to the officer now. The patrolman indicated some additional facts by Scott's contact information, such as: *discovered the body; was a former crime scene investigator in Louisville, KY; on PI case in Gatlinburg.* Handing Scott back his license, the officer indicated that he was free to go as well, but Scott stayed put.

The fact that Scott was still present did not escape Carter's watchful eye. The lieutenant eyeballed Scott on and off, as the crime scene turned into a flurry of activity. He noted that Scott scrutinized every detail of what the crime scene team was doing, his head turning to and fro. Scott watched the crime scene photographer snap picture after picture. He watched Lt. Jetro gather, bag, and number evidence, and Scott's eyes were transfixed as the deceased's body was carefully hoisted from the bridge.

Numerous photos were taken of the cavern in the man's back – his likely cause of death – and a few were snapped of the victim's handcuffed hands. Then the body was gradually turned and laid in an open body bag. As the face of the victim came into view, Carter gasped and the medical examiner's eyes bugged. Their shock might have been induced by a number of factors: the near decapitating knife gash across the man's throat; his eerie, cloudy, open eyes; or the murder weapon that was lodged where the man's testicles should have been. But these facts were not what had them so rattled. The dead man's face was what had them stunned.

They recognized the departed as actor Jameson Thornton. As this disturbing fact registered with Carter, the lieutenant found himself glancing up at Scott to gage his reaction. Carter fully expected to see astonishment on Scott's face as well, but he was surprised to see that Scott did not look shocked by the celebrity status of the victim. The lieutenant found this item of interest to be very strange, and he always filed strange reactions away in his brain for future reference.

As news teams arrived, further snarling traffic along the Parkway, and it was learned that the dead man was famed actor Jameson Thornton, a media frenzy began to erupt. Scott decided it was time to take his exit before some reporter stuck a microphone and a camera in his face. He did not want his wife Sherri to find out about his escapades on the news. Scott clandestinely slipped away to his van, but his departure did not elude the attentiveness of Lt. Jetro.

That man knows more than he told me, Carter's gut screamed. The lieutenant had long ago learned that his gut was seldom wrong. He was certain he and Scott Arnold would meet, and talk, again in the very near future.

Chapter 2

Heavy on the Mind

Scott pulled his van into the driveway of his wife Sherri's Hendersonville, Tennessee home – also his home now – around two p.m. He pulled up behind Sherri's black Buick LeSabre. Twenty-seven-year-old Sherri, a homicide investigator with the Hendersonville Police Department for almost three years, had worked the night shift the evening before – eleven p.m. until eight a.m. – so Scott realized she might likely be sleeping right now.

Scott was two years older than Sherri. He and Sherri had met, nearly a year ago, when Scott had come to Hendersonville to consult with Sherri on a homicide case that he had been working as a private investigator. The homicide in question was very similar to several cases Scott had worked when he had been a homicide investigator in Louisville, Kentucky, a year and a half before.

The last thing either Scott or Sherri had been looking for was a romantic entanglement. Sherri had recently divorced and Scott still suffered heartbreak over the death of his beloved girlfriend, one of the homicides he had been investigating in Louisville. He and Sherri had intended to maintain a professional relationship only; both working toward the same goal of bringing a killer to justice. But undeniable physical attraction and highly compatible personalities had slammed, and held, them together like magnets. Scott could not imagine his life without Sherri now.

Unlocking the front door, he slipped into their house, taking care not to rattle his keys and pulling the storm door closed instead of allowing it slam. The house was quiet except for the hum of the furnace and the refrigerator running. Scott went into the empty kitchen and bestowed his keys and wallet on the corner of the table. He took off his jacket and hung it on the back of a chair. Then he slipped off his shoes before leaving the kitchen and taking light steps down the carpeted hallway toward the bedroom.

Opening the bedroom door, Scott spied Sherri lying in their bed. Her eyes were closed and she was curled on her side with a light tan blanket pulled to her chin. Strands of dark brown hair covered her cheek and the top of the blanket. Scott approached the bed, gently brushed the hair from Sherri's cheek and bent to bestow a warm kiss on her soft rosy skin.

Sherri stirred and her light brown eyes fluttered open. As she focused, and Scott's face came into view, a glorious smile graced her wide ruby lips. "Hi," she mumbled in a voice still drowsy with sleep. "Why don't you try that on my mouth?" she teased as she became more awake.

"I'd love to," Scott told her, his lips widening into a smile of their own. He wasted little time before touching those same lips to Sherri's. Scott loved kissing this woman. He was a very happily married newlywed; he and Sherri had been married only two months.

When the kiss ended, Sherri said, "I been waitin' on that. I thought I'd get my kisses this mornin' when I slipped into the warm bed with you. Them…and maybe a bit more…," she said with a naughty grin and dancing, devilish eyes.

"Is that so?" Scott said, giving her another kiss. This one packed more heat. "Well…I could fix that. And now… here you are all rested. Whereas before…you would have been tired. Maybe it was a good thing that I was gone when you came home this morning."

"May…be," Sherri agreed with a snicker. Then with a creased brow, she asked, "Why'd ya git such an early start this mornin' anyway? Ya had to have left the house before eight thirty, and usually ya aren't even outta bed at that time. What was so import'nt this mornin'?" She questioned, her large eyes inquisitive.

Scott knew that what Sherri said was true. Since he set his own hours, these hours, as a rule, rarely began before about ten a.m. So Scott understood why Sherri was so curious about his day starting so much earlier. But Scott did not want to talk about Gatlinburg. He realized he would eventually have to broach the subject, but right now he had other things on his mind.

"Why don't we talk later?" he suggested with a crocked grin. "I think I owe you some more kisses. And…maybe a bit more."

"I like the way ya think, Mr. Arnold," Sherri agreed. Peeling back the cover, she suggested, "Why don't ya climb in bed with me. It's warm."

"I like the way you think too, Mrs. Arnold," Scott said with a pleased leer and climbed into bed with his wife, sliding her toasty body into his arms and smothering her lips with pursuing, impassioned kisses.

* * * *

Euphoric and relaxed, Scott fell into an easy slumber after their lovemaking. His subconscious soon disturbed his peaceful sleep though, pulling him back in time six months to a harrowing incident he longed to forget.

Scott was standing on a railroad bridge in Nashville, Tennessee. A pair of handcuffs was around each of his ankles and one of these sets was attached to an anchor driven far into one of the railroad ties. As a train thundered onto the bridge behind him, Scott could feel death bearing down like a closing vice.

Scott struggled like a wild animal, gouging flesh around his ankle into raw meat. He would have sliced off his foot if he had a saw. On the track with him were Sherri and a psychiatrist known as Dr. Wallace Cleaver. They were all tugging with all their might, trying to free Scott. The other pair of handcuffs had been anchored to the track as well, but Dr. Cleaver had managed to dislodge this set.

"Get off the track!" Scott shouted, flailing and waving his arms at Sherri.

Scott could see the blinding light from the train shining in Sherri's sweating, soiled face. Slits where her eyes should have been concealed her beautiful brown irises. Scott could hear the locomotive's earsplitting, screeching brakes and piercing whistle. He could smell the putrid smell of scorching brakes. He thrashed about helpless, awaiting their impending deaths.

"Scott!" he heard Sherri's voice call to him.

He was being shaken back and forth. Scott believed his body tremors were due to the hammering of his heart and the quaking of the railroad ties as the train rumbled onward, bringing them closer to meeting their maker.

"Scott!" he heard again, as he realized his eyes were pinched closed. *I shut them to keep from seeing Sherri get killed*, he thought in horror.

"Scott, honey, it's okay," he heard Sherri utter in a tender, soothing voice. He could also feel her soft fingertips caressing his cheeks.

Scott finally forced his eyes open. When he did, he was surprised to find himself looking *up* into Sherri's *sweat free*, *unsoiled* face. Her bed messed hair was hanging down into his face, tickling his cheeks, and Sherri's large brown eyes stared at him, pools of concern. "It's okay, sweetie," she tried to assure him, bending to impart a consoling kiss on Scott's sweat beaded brow. *"We're* okay. We made it off that track. Ya're just havin' another nightmare about that awful night."

As the last remnants of Scott's nightmare began to fade, he opened his arms and engulfed Sherri in a hug, squeezing her to him. Liking the cozy feel of her naked body pressing against his, Scott's fear abated. Stoking the back of Sherri's head, Scott proclaimed in a shaky voice, "I love you more than I can say!"

Wiggling free from Scott's grasp, Sherri looked him in the eye and said with an affirming grin, "I love you too, Scott."

"That much I could never doubt," he told her, forcing a smile of his own, even though his eyes were much too serious. A variation of the Bible verse: *There is no greater love than to lay down one's life for another,* screamed in Scott's head. Sherri had come so near to giving her life for him that night on the Nashville Railroad Bridge. Scott would never forget this fact, and he would never doubt her love or loyalty to him.

But even though he and Sherri had miraculously survived, Dr. Wallace Cleaver had not been so lucky. Scott shuddered as his mind's eye replayed the gruesome scene of the doctor's body flailing in the air, after being struck by the train, and flying over the side of the bridge. Scott's ears could still hear the splash of the doctor's body in the swift moving current below.

Scott realized he could never take the chance of Sherri being put in harm's way again. That was why he was determined to do anything, and *everything*, in his power to bring down the serial killer that had wreaked havoc in their lives. Scott's nemesis was a man trapped in a woman's body named Jeanette O'Riley Peterson; a.k.a. Debbie Gray; a.k.a. *whatever name he has currently stolen.*

Scott was resolved to see that justice was done no matter how long it took. He would do absolutely anything. Jeanette had to pay for all the pain and suffering – and death – four victims in Kentucky and four in Tennessee – he had inflicted.

"Scott, are you *o*kay?" Sherri asked, raising her head off his shoulder and looking him in the eye again. She did not like how quiet he was being or the grim expression on his face. She knew the gears were still whirling in her husband's mind.

"Of course I'm *ooo*...kay," he assured Sherri, drawing out his 'o' in okay in an attempt to tease Sherri about her strong Southern accent. In actuality, Sherri's accent was just one of the many things he found so charming about her. Before she got aggravated with his mockery, Scott rose up and gave Sherri a peck on the lips. "I'll always be okay as long as I have you in my life. How could I be anything but okay?"

Any aggravation Sherri might have felt about Scott making light of her speech pattern instantly dissipated with Scott's endearing words. "Sweet talk will get ya *everywhare,* Mr. Arnold," Sherri purred with a chuckle, giving Scott another kiss, this one longer and more pursuing. "After all, as far as I'm concerned, we're still honeymoonin'."

"Works for me," Scott agreed, a smile lighting his face for the first time since before his nightmare had shaken him to the core.

As Scott held Sherri in his arms, kissing her, and losing himself to passion once more, all was right with his world. But he knew he must fight to make sure that it stayed this way. This fight meant Jeanette needed to be punished for his crimes. *And so he will be,* Scott pledged, pushing thoughts of this deranged individual aside and focusing solely on pleasing his adored wife.

Chapter 3

Top Story

When Sherri and Scott sat down for dinner at five o'clock that evening, and Sherri flipped on the television on the kitchen counter, the early evening news was just coming on. The camera centered on ABC's Channel 6 news desk and Hanson Jonas, popular grey-haired anchor for this network. Hanson's middle-aged, sky blue eyes looked directly into the camera, and with a grim expression, he rattled off, "And in our top story tonight... Two time Oscar winning actor, Jameson Thornton, was found stabbed to death behind a gift shop in Gatlinburg, Tennessee early this morning. Jan Fargo has more details. Jan?"

Upon hearing this information, Sherri's head snapped up from her dinner plate of spaghetti and meatballs. Her attention was suddenly riveted to the television instead. The cameras had switched to Jan Fargo.

Curly-headed, dark-haired Jan, bundled up in a red winter jacket with the ABC logo and Channel 6 printed on the right-hand side, held a microphone up to her mouth, saying, "Hanson, I'm standing across the street from the Hemp Shop and Morton's Antiques in Gatlinburg, Tennessee." The camera swung to a view of these two stores. Since it was already growing dark, there was not a lot to see. The cameraman focused his lens back on Jan and she continued, "A little after eight this morning, a body was discovered by some tourists hanging from the footbridge beside Morton's Antiques. One tourist called the Gatlinburg P.D. Upon closer inspection, the individual was deemed to be actor Jameson Thornton."

Scott was surprised, and a bit relieved, to hear himself referred to as merely a tourist. As he raised his glass and swallowed a swig of the soft drink he was drinking, he watched as the cameras switched back to the studio and Hanson Jonas' somber face.

"Jan, do Gatlinburg P.D. have any leads yet on who could have perpetrated such a heinous crime?" Hanson asked, a deep, disapproving frown on his face.

"No. Not yet, Hanson. They told me they would keep us posted as details unravel," Jan replied as the camera focused on her once more. "Jameson Thornton was a wonderful actor. He will be greatly missed by all," she added with sad, downcast eyes.

"Indeed," Hanson was quick to agree, as the camera swept back to the station. "Thank you, Jan," he said, before announcing, "We have a video montage we would like to play for Jameson Thornton now."

As the song, *I Will Remember You* by Sarah McLachlin played, clips and pictures from Jameson career were flashed upon the screen. It began with Jameson as an eighteen year old heartthrob when he had starred on a popular 1976 television series called *West Coast*. Then clips and pictures from each of his movies – nine to be exact – were quickly scrolled across the screen. The montage ended with a blank, light blue screen with **Jameson Thornton** (1958-2008) in big, black, bold lettering.

The studio switched back to Hanson Jonas, and in a deep voice with sorrowful eyes, he stated, "Jameson Thornton is survived by his daugher, Alana O'Malley, and his grandson, Patrick Alan O'Malley. May Jameson Thornton rest in peace.

As Jan said earlier, he will be missed by all." He briefly paused, and then added, "We'll be right back."

As a series of commercials was aired, Sherri looked at Scott with stunned eyes and commented, "Wow! I cain't believe such a brutal murder happened in quiet lil' Gatlinburg."

"Yeah. Me either," Scott replied, looking down at his plate as he swirled his fork in his spaghetti. Scott was struggling to decide whether or not he should reveal to Sherri all he knew about Jameson Thornton's murder.

Sticking a fork full of food into his mouth and chewing, Scott looked back up at Sherri. She was also chewing up some food and looking at the television again.

There's no real sense in upsetting her, Scott quickly decided. *I'll tell Sherri everything down the road, once I have good news to report*, he concluded, settling back in his chair, intent on sharing a carefree dinner with his wife.

Chapter 4

The Details

Jameson Thornton's Gatlinburg security guard, a vertically-challenged, slightly overweight man with short, spiked, blond hair and greenish-brown eyes, shared his grief with Christopher Nelson, Jameson Thornton's agent/manager. "This shouldn't have happened, Mr. Nelson," he told the older man, biting his lip and shaking his head. "I tried to persuade Jameson not to go into town alone..."

"You should have followed him," Christopher chastised, raking a hand through his auburn grey hair. "Your job was to stay on his tail." Jameson Thornton had been a steady source of income for Christopher for many years, and he was not happy that Jameson had died so young.

"What more can I say? I'm sorry," the security officer apologized, loudly exhaling and looking down at his feet.

Christopher also studied the ground, shaking his head. He knew that Jameson had long been a wild card. Because of his arrogance, Jameson was known to do stupid things from time to time, like ditching his security guards. *His stupidity got him killed this time*, Christopher ascertained, aggravated.

"Mr. Nelson, I know it's asking a lot, but I'd like to pay my final respects to Jameson. Can you let me know the particulars on when and where Jameson will be laid out?" the repentent guard asked.

Christopher's anger with this local security official faded as quickly as if had arisen. After years of working with

Jameson Thornton, Christopher knew firsthand how extremely difficult Jameson could be. "Sure. I'll send you an e-mail with all the particulars once everything is all worked out," Christopher told this other man.

"That would be swell!" the guard chirped, the first trace of a smile of his face. This man would eagerly await an e-mail from Christopher, and once he had the particulars, he fully intended to share these details with one other very important person.

* * * *

A few days later, when Scott retrieved the mail from the mailbox, he discovered a plain white envelope addressed to him with no return address on it.

Curious, Scott headed to the kitchen, took a knife, stuck it in a small gap under the flap and tore open the envelope. The knife jangled as he tossed it aside in the sink. Then Scott reached inside the envelope. Papers rattled as he pulled forth the contents and unfolded two sheets of paper. Eyeballing these items, Scott discovered one was a typewritten note and the other was handwritten.

Scott's heart rate quickened as he read both items. *Jeanette, what do you have planned this time?* he wondered with uttermost frustration.

Scott gathered his keys from the kitchen table. He suddenly needed to go and talk to a travel agent.

Chapter 5

The Honeymooners

Sherri had just gotten home from work – a normal shift: eight a.m. until five p.m. She had no sooner stuck her key in the front lock than Scott unlocked the door from inside. Pulling it open, he stepped back so Sherri could come inside. An ear-to-ear smile covered his face and his hands were behind his back.

"What's up?" Sherri asked, returning his smile. Her eyes trailed from Scott's face to his arms. "What have ya got behind yer back, Mr. Arnold?" Sherri stuck her keys in her purse and sat her bag on a side table. She also unbuttoned her coat.

"Behind my back?" Scott questioned. A flash of mischief lightened his darker brown eyes.

"Yeah…behind…yer back," Sherri said, lunging at him. Scott stumbled back several paces as Sherri reached around his body and her hands snapped upon the envelope that Scott held in his hands. Scott allowed it to slip free.

Sherri pulled the envelope around the side of his body. When she had it in front of her, she looked down at it and then reached to pull two slips of paper out of a slit on the side. Looking up at Scott with surprise, she uttered, "These are plane tickets to Los Angeles. What gives?"

"I think it's time we get away for a real honeymoon," Scott surprised her by saying. "I need to go to L.A. to do a little PI work, so I thought I would combine business with…well…pleasure. So what do you say, Mrs. Arnold. Want to go to L.A. for a few days with your handsome, irresistible husband?"

"L.A.? Are ya serious?" Sherri asked, glancing at the tickets again and then looking back into Scott's beaming face. She was pleased and rattled all at the same time. She had not even had a chance to take her coat off yet. "I'd like to go, Scott, but what about Angela?" Angela was Sherri's four-year-old daughter from her previous marriage.

"I've talked to George, and he is going to keep her while we're gone," Scott told his wife. Sherri and George, Sherri's ex-husband and Angela's father, shared joint custody of Angela, so Angela usually spent a few days at her mom's house and then a few days at her dad's.

"Sounds like ya've got this all planned out," Sherri said, giving Scott an approving smile. She placed her arms around his neck and drew in for a kiss.

"I do. I've even spoken to Captain Lafferty, and he said you are due a vacation. So all you need to do is pack, and we'll be off in a few days. It's time we had an 'official' honeymoon," Scott said with bedroom eyes and a chuckle, kissing her again.

"I love ya, Mr. Arnold," Sherri gushed, squeezing their bodies together in a hug and kissing the side of Scott's neck. "I can't wait for our 'official' honeymoon to start."

"Me either," Scott agreed. "But it will have to wait. Because Angela's in her room. I thought you would like to spend some time with your daughter before we left."

"As I said, ya thought of everythang," Sherri purred, a delighted grin playing at the corners of her mouth. Sherri loved Scott a great deal. She truly could not wait for their time alone in Los Angeles to begin. But for now, she pulled away, took off her coat, hung it in the closet, and made off down the hall, with Scott, to spend some quality time with her precious little girl.

* * * *

Jameson Thornton's body was laid out, for family and more importantly, fan viewing, in the center of Beverly Gardens Park. Beverly Gardens Park, a two-mile strip running the complete length of the city of Beverly Hills, bordered fourteen blocks of Santa Monica Boulevard. Rose gardens, ornate stone park benches, a lily pond, fountains, tall trees, and a unique cactus garden beautified Jameson's choice of location for his viewing.

Known for wearing wide ascots instead of ties, this fashion statement came in handy for Jameson at his showing, because the ascot circumspectly covered his vile neck wound. Jameson's body was outlined by, cushy, flowing, burgundy silk and rested in a massive, gleaming Brazilian cherry casket with glistening gold handles and the outline of an Oscar, carved in the top.

Those arriving to pay their respects stood in the bright California sunshine and shuffled along a gravel path usually used by joggers. Multitudes of police and security officers, and strategically placed barricades, lined the way between the walking path and the street, keeping the thousands of fans and curious onlookers in line. A continuous stream of people waited in line to promenade past Jameson's casket, say some parting words, and perhaps leave a memento in his casket or along the ground around it. One of these people was Scott Arnold.

* * * *

As Scott edged along with the excited crowd, he tuned out all of the useless chitter-chatter going on all around him. A woman's strong perfume irritated his nostrils, and had Scott wondering if she hoped her scent would rouse Jameson Thornton from the dead. Scott attempted to ignore this unpleasant distraction as well.

Scott's primary focus was on surveying his surroundings. He allowed his eyes to make a continuous sweep of the park, studying individuals that happened to linger there. Scott also gave vigilant notice to the faces of the policemen and security officers that stood watch along the walkway and throughout the park. No one gave Scott cause for concern. Everyone there either seemed to be a family member, fan of Jameson Thornton, or someone hired to secure the scene. This fact disappointed Scott a great deal. He wondered why he was here and wished he could leave, but he continued to move at a snail's pace along with the crowd, growing closer and closer to Jameson Thornton's casket.

When Scott finally received his turn at approaching the casket, he slowly moved forward, looking out the corners of his eyes at people standing around him. He still saw no one that alarmed him.

Walking up to the front of the casket, Scott looked down at Jameson Thornton. Just like all corpses in a funeral home, Jameson's face was packed with makeup to give it color, his lips were sealed and stretched into a tight, unnatural line, and his hands were folded one over the top of the other.

Scott was about to walk away when an item of interest caught, and held, his attention. Scott reached to touch Jameson's folded hands, an act that looked like a sweet expression of sympathy to the waiting, and on looking, crowd. But when Scott extracted his hand, he clandestinely took with him a most interesting memento.

Stepping away, Scott allowed his eyes one last, thorough, scan of the people milling about. Then he hurried away toward his rental car.

* * * *

About ten minutes later, a short, blond-haired man stepped from the line and approached Jameson's casket. When he looked down at Jameson's folded hands, he smiled.

It's gone. Mission accomplished, he concluded with tingling excitement.

He moved away, a spring in his step, allowing the next person in line to approach Jameson and pay their final respects. This man headed away to his return car too.

* * * *

When Scott got back from Jameson's showing, he headed straight to his and Sherri's hotel room. When he entered the room, he found it empty. A wave of anxiety, bordering on panic, momentarily swept over Scott. Then his eyes came to rest on a hotel notepad propped up in front of the television. Scott snatched up the pad, and relief swept over him as he discovered a handwritten note from Sherri. Her note told Scott that she was at the pool.

It's time to start enjoying my honeymoon, he told himself. Scott's business in the L.A. area had been concluded, so now, he could focus all of his energy and attention on his personal time. So, with a smile, Scott slipped out of his jeans and polo shirt and into some swimming trunks and headed with a bounce in his step to the pool.

Chapter 6

Back Home

A lovely little girl with mounds of short ebony curls; long lashes; and big, innocent, golden-brown eyes stared up at the man standing beside her twin bed. The man looked down upon the four-year-old child with warmhearted adoring eyes.

Reaching to pull a pink blanket over the girl's petite body, the man said in a quiet, soothing voice, "How's daddy's girl? Daddy missed you while he was gone, but I'm home now."

"I missed you too…um…" The girl stuttered, looking a bit unsure. Her teeth gnawed at her lower lip as she forced herself to continue. "D…daddy."

"That's right! I'm your daddy," the man praised, opening his arms and pulling the child into an approving hug. "Good night, precious. Sleep tight."

"Night, daddy," she said, giving him a slight grin as he released her. Tired, the little girl rolled over on her side, popping her thumb into her mouth.

The man reached underneath a Barbie lampshade to extinguish the child's bedside lamp. But before he left the room, he bent to turn on a seashell night light. Standing in the open doorway of the girl's bedroom, he listened to the girl's even breathing as she slipped into a peaceful sleep.

I'm glad she's finally accepting me as her daddy, he pondered. A pleased smile tugged at the corners of his mouth as he softly closed the child's bedroom door and made his way to the bathroom to take a shower before going to bed.

* * * *

Scott stood in the hallway outside his bedroom door and watched as his wife Sherri shut Angela's bedroom door and make her way toward him.

"Waitin' for me?" she asked with a toothy grin, sliding her arms around Scott's waist.

As Sherri drew in close to him, she inhaled Scott's fresh, clean scent. Noting his black hair was wet and he wore only pajama bottoms, Sherri guessed Scott must have just gotten out of the shower.

"Is Angela all settled in for the night?" Scott asked, giving his wife a fleeting kiss.

"Didn't ya stick yer head in and say goodnight to her?" Sherri asked, releasing Scott and reaching to open their bedroom door. She stepped inside the bedroom, and Scott followed, shutting the door behind him.

"Yeah. I tucked Angela in and told her goodnight before I went to take my shower," Scott told Sherri. Then with a relieved thankful smile, he shared, "I think Angela is starting to accept me as her stepdad. She told me she missed me while I was gone."

"I told ya it wouldn't take long," Sherri said, a wide grin lighting her face.

Since Angela was so young – she would turn five in a few days – Sherri believed Angela and Scott, in time, would develop a close relationship. Nothing would please Sherri more. After all, she loved Scott a great deal and wanted Angela to love Scott as well, and Sherri knew Scott already cared a great deal for her daughter – bordering on thinking of her as his own child.

"So tell me, Mr. Arnold, isn't it about time we got to bed too?" Sherri asked with a twinkle in her eye, holding out a hand to him.

"Oh, yeah! Past time!" he agreed with hearty enthusiasm. Scott took Sherri's hand and allowed her to lead him toward the bed. He had enjoyed their time alone in Los Angeles, but Scott was glad to be home with Sherri and Angela. *My family*, he mused with contentment.

Chapter 7

Calls

Two weeks later, on a Friday, an unknown man came into the tiny, stale, dimly lit office of the Adam Ridge Motel. Adam Ridge was a small, ill-reputed – rates by the hour – establishment with only ten rooms, located on the far outskirts of Pigeon Forge, Tennessee. Needless to say, Adam Ridge was *not* frequented by tourists.

Hearing the bell on the desk ding, the clerk, a large man in worn jeans with a chain hanging from the pocket and a black muscle shirt came out of a room in the back and approached the front desk with a cigarette hanging out of his mouth. This man had long grey hair that was pulled back in a braided ponytail, and his burly arms were completely covered by a colorful variety of tatoos.

"Can I hep ya?" he asked, blowing a cloud of sour smoke in the stranger's direction.

"I'm hoping you can," the visitor replied, a lopsided grin on his face. Pulling forth his wallet, this man extracted a fifty dollar bill. "I need some information," he revealed, holding the bill up where the clerk could see it.

"What kinda informat'n?" the clerk asked, eyeballing the money.

"There's a couple who show up here a lot on Friday and hook up in room 105. I need to find out their names. The guy's an average Joe but the gal that joins him is a succulent blonde about half his age. Can you help me?" the guest asked, laying the money on the corner of the desk now. He held his fingers only on the edge.

SISSY MARLYN

Taking one last puff from his cigarette and exhaling more smoke in his visitor's direction, the clerk pulled the butt from his mouth and ground it out in a stained, metal ashtray on the countertop. Reaching under the counter, this man pulled forth a register book. Adam Ridge did things the old-fashioned way; no computerized guest records for this establishment.

Plopping the register book on the countertop, the clerk opened it and thumbed to the previous Friday. "Well...looks like ya weren't too far off," he told the stranger with an idiotic smile. When his guest gave him a puzzled look, he expounded, "Ya said the guy was an average *Joe*, and ya was right on the mark. The guy's name is Joe Butler, and his lil' tart's name is Jennifer. Don't know her last name, but I'm willin' to bet it ain't Butler."

"I'm quite certain you're right," the visitor agreed, smiling and letting loose of the fifty.

The clerk quickly reached to snap up the bill and immediately pocketed it. "Ya cain't let on that I gave ya the informat'n I jest did; is that understood?" he asked, sticking out his chest.

"My lips," the stranger said, putting his fingers up to his mouth. "Are sealed," he stated, moving his fingers along his lips as if zipping them.

"Nice doin' business with ya," the clerk said, smiling widely and showing yellow, chipped teeth.

"Likewise," his visitor said. Then this man turned, stepped over some broken linoleum and slipped out of the office.

* * * *

A short while later, Scott's cell phone rang. "Hello," he answered, his voice very serious. Scott's caller ID had not identified the caller, so Scott was on instant alert.

"Hello, Scott," the caller said. It was a muffled female voice.

"Who's calling?" he asked, suspicious. The voice sounded much the same as the caller who had phoned to tell him about Jameson Thornton's murder.

"Um..." she replied in a low growl. "Let's just call me the fortune teller, shall we? Would you like to hear your fortune for today?"

"I really don't have time for games," Scott snapped. "What have you done this time?"

"I haven't done anything...*yet*," she replied; further teasing, "Maybe I *will* do something or maybe I *won't*. The only way to find out for sure would be for you to go to the Adam Ridge Motel, room 105. I'd suggest you leave *now!*"

"Adam Ridge Motel, room 105?" Scott repeated. This specific hotel gave Scott reason for worry, and the room number gave him cause for even greater concern.

"That's right. Head there now, Scott. After all, it's a three-and-a-half hour drive for you. It might be a matter of life...or death," she said, snickering.

"Jeanette, you SOB," Scott swore. But there was only silence on the other end of the line now. When Scott pulled his cell phone away from his ear, the flashing display read: Call Ended.

Scott snapped his phone closed and shoved it in his pocket. His keys jingled as he snatched them from the table and bolted for his front door. Slamming and locking the door behind him, Scott hurried to his awaiting van.

* * * *

A few hours later, when Joe Butler's cell phone rang, he expected it to be his girlfriend calling to arrange their little get-together. Fifty-five-year-old Joe drove a truck for a living, and

Friday was his day off. So while his wife was off at work, Joe got together at a local motel with a much younger woman, named Jennifer, for some much needed, physical, stress relief.

"Hilloo," Joe answered his phone, sounding chipper.

"Hi, Joe," a sultry female voice replied.

Joe waited a moment for the caller to identify herself, and when he got nothing but continuing silence, he asked, "Who is this?"

"I'm a friend of Jennifer's," the woman replied.

"Yeah? What's up?" Joe asked, wondering with trepidation why Jennifer would have one of her friends call him.

"Well...let's just say I know what I'd like to be up," the unknown called said, breathing deeply. "I wanted to know if I could join you and Jennifer in your room today. Jennifer says you're man enough for both of us. Is she shitting me, or is this true?"

"Oh, it's definitely true," Joe confirmed, stroking his own ego. Joe knew he was no male Adonis. His arms, legs, and face were too long. He had a bit of a beer belly, a bad receding hairline, and a big nose.

"Well..." she said, drawing in another deep, trembling breath. "How about you meet us in about twenty minutes at the usual place, and we'll find out," the caller suggested.

"I can do that," Joe said with confidence, hoping this call was not a joke.

The breathy female on the other end of the line said, "Looking forward to it. We'll see you in a few."

"See ya," Joe said, as their connection was broken. *Well, if Jennifer wants a twosome, I'm certainly up to the challenge*, he mused.

Joe left the house and headed directly for Adam Ridge Motel.

* * * *

Arriving at the Adam Ridge Motel about ten minutes later, Joe checked in, renting his usual room for two hours. Going directly to the room, Joe unlocked the door and opened it to a dark room. He switched on the dome light in the entry foyer and stepped inside. It was a sunny day outside, so Joe could have opened the drapes and brightened the room, but he purposedly left the dingy beige drapes closed.

Closing the door, Joe inhaled the familar, musty smell of the room. Taking off his coat, he caused a few old metal hangers to sing a jangling tune as he reached to extract one from a coat rack just inside the door. Placing his coat on the hanger, Joe hung up his jacket. There were two thuds as he kicked off his shoes and also left them in this area, out of the way of foot traffic.

Walking along tattered carpet over to the King-sized bed, Joe reached to grab the remote from a table beside the bed. Plopping down on top of the worn bedspread, Joe leaned against the headboard. Pushing the power button on the remote, he watched as the outdated nineteen-inch television flashed on. He selected an adult movie from an onscreen menu.

Joe was relaxing on the bed, watching his movie, and growing aroused when he heard a knock on the door. *Just in time girls!*, he thought with relish, salivating as he bounced off the bed and made quick tracks toward the door.

Joe thrust the door open without even looking to see who it was. Instead of finding his date – or dates – Joe was surprised when he found a short, pudgy, blond-haired man in a security uniform standing on the threshold of his room.

It did not take the security guard long to convince Joe to let him come into his room.

Chapter 8

Disturbing Discovery

Pulling his blue Econoline van into the badly maintained, compact, parking lot of the Adam Ridge Motel, Scott attempted to dodge the Grand Canyon of potholes. Scott's latest client's husband, Joe Butler, patronized this motel quite a lot. A blond-haired woman, half Joe's age, often met this man at this location. Scott's task was to take photographs of this wanton couple and send the pictures back to Joe's wife to prove her husband's infidelity. Scott hated these assignments, but he had long since learned to tolerate them. Such was the life of a private investigator.

Scott spied Joe Butler's familiar white Ford Expedition pulled into the parking spot in front of Joe and his young girlfriend's usual room, 105. Scott pulled his van into a parking space nearby. Putting the van into park, Scott killed the ignition, silencing the new Eagles CD he had been listening to on the over three-and-a-half hour drive there.

Scott extracted his keys and reached to pull his door handle. His door swung open with a slight screech that alerted Scott, yet again, that his door hinges needed oil. Stepping out of the van, Scott closed the door and walked forward toward the slightly raised, concrete pad that ran in front of the rooms.

Stepping up onto the walkway, Scott lumbered toward the warped door with a rusty 105 on it. As Scott passed by the dirty window to this room, he was surprised to find the drapes standing open. Taking advantage of the unshielded window,

Scott peered inside the room. The threadbare bedspread on the king-sized bed was crumpled as if someone had sat, or lain, on it, and Scott could see the flash of naked bodies on the television, indicating that Joe had a porn movie playing. But Scott saw no sign of Joe or his girlfriend.

As Scott stepped closer to the door, he found it slightly ajar. Considering it was the first day of December and quite nippy outside, Scott found it more than a little odd that the door was not closed completely. He placed his hand against the door and silently pushed it open.

Slipping into the room, Scott's nose picked up the sour smell of old cigarette smoke. He tiptoed along frayed carpet between the bed and the television. Scott gave the naked, rocking, panting and moaning porn stars the slightest of glances. He was focused on finding Joe Butler. Steady pinpricks along his spine, and old police instinct, told Scott something was not right.

As he approached the bathroom door, he discovered that it too was not completely closed. Steam curled from under the door and through the crack along the side, and Scott could hear a shower running. He breathed a sigh of relief, considering, *Maybe I missed their tryst today, and Joe is just taking a shower and cleaning up afterwards.* But as soon as this thought registered, Scott instantly doubted, *What would be the point of the call on my cell phone telling me to be here if it's that simple?*

Scott closed the rest of the distance between him and the bathroom door. He placed his palm in the center of the door and found it warm and damp. *So the shower's been running for a while,* he concluded, reaching with his other hand to stroke his stiffening neck.

Scott hesitated for a moment more, and then he gradually opened the door. A hot mist lapped at his face and body. Rolls of steam rushed past him, escaping into the much cooler adjoining room. Scott peered through the haze and saw glimpses of a closed, light brown shower curtain.

Drawing closer to the tub, Scott strained his ears, listening for sounds of movement from within the shower – feet moving, humming, singing, and/or soap, shampoo or razors being placed along a porcelain ledge. But other than the surge and splash of water, he detected nothing.

Standing beside the plain, thin plastic, shower curtain, as the steam began to clear, Scott could see no faint outline of movement in the tub either. He reached to grasp the shower curtain and gave it a quick tug sideways. As metal rings sang a jingling tune, Scott hoped to come face to face with a stunned Joe Butler.

Joe's stunned eyes did meet with Scott's, but not in the manner Scott had hoped. His lifeless, wide, open eyes stared up at Scott and the moist ceiling above. Joe was lying on his back, fully clothed, in the tub amongst chunks of his gory flesh and streams of red.

Joe's blood also coated the inside of the shower curtain and the walls. Plentiful red streaks and spatter provided the peeling, drab, tan, wallpaper with a new, eerie design. Water, ricocheting off of Joe's chest and handcuffed hands, cleansed the horrific gaping crevice where his neck should have been. Joe's pants and underwear had been pulled down; his genitals looked as if they had been milled into ground beef; and this area served as a depository for a knife – the obvious murder weapon.

"Good God!" Scott exclaimed, dropping his head into a hand and shaking it. "Not again!"

Scott stumbled backwards, intent on sitting on the cracked toilet seat lid, since his legs felt weak and his stomach sick. But before he could lower himself, Scott heard movement in the other room. On instant alert, Scott reached into his pocket and fingered the handle of a gun. *You won't have the upper hand this time, Jeanette*, he was determined.

As he took a step toward the door, Scott heard, "Police! Come out with your hands up."

Scott stepped sideways and peeked into the adjoining room. Seeing a uniformed Pigeon Forge officer, he extracted his hand from his pocket. Placing both hands high in the air, he inched out of the room.

"Officer, I was just about to call you," Scott said, as he stood face to face with him.

"Is that so?" the policeman asked, approaching Scott and beginning to pat him down.

When the officer's hand made contact with Scott's jacket pocket, his hand dived inside and whisked out Scott's gun. He waved it in the air, like a trophy. Then he swiftly handed it to the gloved officer beside him, who bagged it as if it were evidence of some crime. Another policeman stood just inside the room by the closed entrance door, but this officer seemed more interested in watching the porn movie than in seeing to his fellow patrolmen's actions or Scott's.

"I have a concealed carry license," Scott explained, as the officer with his gun passed him, going into the bathroom. Scott rattled on, "My name is Scott Arnold. I'm a private investigator. I was here on a case. But…well…the man I was investigating is in the bathroom tub. He's been murdered."

A moment later, the policeman, who had passed Scott, came back out of the bathroom. Pointing behind him with his thumb, he confirmed, "Yep. Sure 'nough, there's a stiff in 'da bathtub. Pretty carved up."

"Spin around and put yer hands behind yer back, please," the officer facing Scott requested.

"Behind...my...my back?" Scott questioned, his eyes looking bewildered.

"Yes, sir," the officer said, looking impatient and twirling his finger in front of him.

Scott reluctantly did as requested, finding himself facing the other policeman that still stood in the bathroom door holding Scott's gun in a bag. Scott began to get a bad taste in his mouth about what was going down. It appeared much too much as if he were a murder suspect and not just someone that had innocently discovered a dead man.

Scott's fears were confirmed when he felt the policeman behind him tugging his arms back and the cold steel of handcuffs touching his wrists. Hearing the cuffs snap closed, Scott ears picked up the all too familiar words that he himself had uttered on numerous occasions: "Mr. Arnold, yer under arrest for the murder of Joe Butler. Ya have the right to remain silent...."

"I know my rights, officer," he interrupted, glancing over his shoulder. Then Scott clarified, "I was a police officer myself."

"Okay. Suit yerself," the officer replied, happy not to have to rattle on with the Miranda rights.

As Scott felt the policeman's hand clasp his upper arm to turn him, something odd in the officer's statement dawned on him. "How did you know the victim's name?" Scott questioned, wondering all at once how it was that the police just happened to show up at this particular moment.

"We're here on an anonymous tip," the officer shared. He exerted slight pressure on Scott's arm, prodding him to turn.

"Well, doesn't that just figure," Scott commented under his breath, shaking his head as the policeman started walking him toward the door and the awaiting squad car.

Scott suddenly felt very foolish. He realized he had walked right into a well-conceived trap. And to make matters worse, Scott was certain his fingerprints were on the front door, the bathroom door, and the shower curtain.

Being arrested for murder was not a twist Scott had expected in his wildest imagination, but yet here he was being loaded into the back of a Pigeon Forge squad car. *Jeanette, you son of a bitch, you won't get away with this*, Scott silently pledged as he was driven away in a police vehicle, headed for the Pigeon Forge Police Department and an awaiting interrogation room.

Chapter 9

Gloating

A man sat in a chair, by the window, in room 205, directly across the parking lot from Joe's room. He had specifically requested this room, because it gave him a great vantage point for observing what transpired in Joe's room. He had the curtain parted just enough to peek his nose out now, and he liked what he saw.

The man's sharp hazel eyes watched as one of three Pigeon Forge police officers came out of Joe's room. This policeman was leading Scott Arnold, in handcuffs, to his nearby police cruiser.

"Ye...es!" the voyager cheered.

Shaking his hands fisted in the air, he allowed the curtain to slip from his grasp and fully close. *My plan is working brilliantly!* he ascertained with utmost satisfaction. *Scott is jumping through hoops like a trained circus tiger.*

As he pulled apart the curtain and peered out again, he saw the police car, with Scott inside, pulling out of a parking space and heading toward the exit of the motel. Allowing the curtain to close once more, he allowed himself a little time to savor all the wonderous things he had accomplished.

He thought about what a fool Joe Butler had been. *I can't believe that moron let me in the room so easily*, he mused. *All I had to say was I needed to check his room for a missing teenage girl. He just assumed I was with hotel security. He never asked to see an ID or anything. He made murdering him so easy. Fools and scumbags like him deserve to die. Each time I kill someone like Joe Butler, I do the world a favor*, he concluded.

He closed his eyes and re-envisioned his encounter with Joe again with utmost satisfaction.

Once inside Joe's room, behind a closed door, I pulled my trusty gun out of my jacket pocket. "Why don't we take a little walk to the bathroom?" I strongly suggested.

Staring at the gun, Joe raised his hands and pleaded his case, "Look, pal, I don't know what ya're after. But I've only got about five bucks in my wallet. If you're here to rob me, ya've picked the wrong room. And I'm expectin' company any minute. They'll know I'm here because they know that's my SUV outside. They'll know somethin's wrong if I don't answer the door."

"Is that so?" I asked, smiling. In a spicy female voice, I asked, "So do you think you can handle the two of us, Joe?"

"Wh...?" Joe uttered. "That was you that called me? How'd ya git my number? Did Jennifer give it to ya?"

"Anywho.com, Joe. Great website; lots of great info, Joe," I replied with an amused grin. All I had needed was Joe's name and address, and I had gotten both; his address from following Scott around and his name from the helpful motel clerk I had bribed.

"Is this some kinda sick joke? It ain't really funny if it is," Joe stated.

"I can assure you, Joe, that this isn't a joke," I told him, all seriousness now. "I've enjoyed our little catch up, but now it's time for you to do as I ask. Head to the bathroom, please. I'd hate to have to shoot you, but I can assure you that I will if you don't start moving... Now!" I commanded, thrushing the gun out closer and shaking it.

Joe had the nerve to try and settle me, saying, "Okay, pal. Don't git excited." Still holding his hands high in the air, he shook his long, gangly arms back and forth. *"I'll go into the bathroom if ya want. No big deal,"* he agreed, turning. Walking in that direction, he said, *"Ya can have my wallet, even though it don't have a lot in it, like I done told ya."*

Once in the bathroom, I reached in my other jacket pocket and pulled forth a pair of handcuffs. *"Here,"* I said, tossing them. They landed with a clank on the grubby linoleum floor at Joe's big feet.

"What're these for?" Joe asked, bending to pick them up. There was a puzzled expression on his long, hound dog face.

"I want you to put your hands out in front of you and click those on," I told him, holding the gun sideways and shaking it.

With a grimace on his face, Joe did as I asked. *"Now, I'm handcuffed and in the bathroom like ya asked. Can ya jest take my wallet now and let me be?"* he asked, his voice a mixture of distress and aggravation.

"Sure," I agreed, with a slight smile. *"Turn around and step into the tub."*

"The tub?" Joe questioned, hard lines forming in his forehead.

"That's what I said. Now do it!" I commanded, taking a step forward with my finger on the trigger of the gun.

"Don't git all mad. I'll git in the tub if that's what ya want," Joe agreed. He turned, walked the short distance to the tub and stepped up over the side. *"See I'm whare ya asked me ta be,"* he pointed out, glancing back. His large nose, shadowing his shoulder, made him look like Jimmy Durante.

"Very good, Joe," I praised, taking a step closer to the tub myself. *"Now kneel down."*

"Look, man, it'll be easier to git my wallet if I'm standin'..."

"Joe...let's not start arguing now," I told him in a stern voice. "Kneel! Now!" I snapped.

Joe slowly lowered himself to a kneeling position.

"Good boy," I praised again, as if I were talking to a dog. Well, he certainly has the face of a dog, I thought with sick humor.

I pounced like a moutain lion on its prey. Slicing and dicing with a large knife I whisked from a pocket inside my jacket. Joe only struggled for a few moments, never getting a chance to scream, because I slashed his throat first.

I laid his limp, blood covered body straight out in the tub. As his crystal blue eyes – with fear locked into them for all eternity – stared up at me, I undid Joe's belt and pulled down his jeans and boxers. I chopped away, again and again, at his most offensive part. "If you don't know how to use it, then lose it," I told him, even though he could no longer hear me. When I was done with this vicious attack, I left my knife sticking out of this region.

I stood and pulled a folded trash bag from another inside pocket of my jacket. Opening the bag, I undressed, placing my blood saturated clothes, including my shoes and socks, inside the bag. The only item of clothing I kept on were my gloves. Turning, I placed the bag out in the floor.

Closing the shower curtain, I looked down at the scars upon my chest and the useless member below my waist. I took a second to wonder why things had to be this way for me. Then I turned on the shower and washed away any residue of Joe's blood from my body and gloves.

Finishing my shower, I turned off the water and grabbed two, off-white, scratchy towels from a nearby rack. Drying my body, I tossed the towels in the floor and stepped out onto them. I reached to grab the garbage bag, and then I walked with the towels under my feet out of the bathroom.

Going over to the bed, I knelt down in the floor. Reaching under the bed, I pulled forth another trash bag that I had placed there a few hours before when I had rented this room for an hour. I knew that the absentee maid service would not locate and extract the bag.

I pulled the bag from the floor and placed it on the bed. Pulling forth items of clothes, I got dressed once more. When I was fully dressed, I pulled off my soaked gloves and tossed them in the trash bag with my other soiled clothes. I also wadded up the sack I had just emptied and placed it in the full bag.

I stooped to pick up one of the motel towels from the floor. Making my way back to the bathroom, I went inside once more. Covering my hand with one of the towels, I turned back on the shower. "We'll clean you all up for Scott Arnold," I said to Joe's corpse, laughing.

I made my way out of the room, pulling the bathroom door closed all but a crack. Walking back over by the bed, I stashed the other motel towel inside my bag. Then I bent to hoist the lone trash sack off the floor. I headed for the door.

Stopping beside the door, with one of the motel towels still around my hand, I reached to pull open the drapes. "It's a sunny day outside. Let's shed some light on this room," I decided, pleased with myself for all I had accomplished.

Clutching the doorknob with the towel, I opened the door. Pulling the door almost closed, I headed off across the parking lot to my room, with the trash bag in hand, to await Scott Arnold's arrival.

I led Scott to Gatlinburg to be at the site of Jameson Thornton's murder. I lured him to Beverly Hills, to Jameson's showing, to further rub Jameson's murder in Scott's face. And *now...crème-de-la-crème... I've gotten Scott arrested for Joe Butler's murder. What a grand day this is!*

Overjoyed, he reared back in his chair by the window and allowed himself to laugh until he nearly cried.

Chapter 10

The Interrogation

At the police station, Scott was immediately led to a small room, with a tan, linoleum floor, plain white walls and dim fluorescent lights in the ceiling. A four-foot table and three metal chairs were the only furniture in the room. A reminiscent smirk played at the corners of Scott's mouth as he was seated in the solitary chair facing the two empty chairs on the other side. *How many times was I seated on the other side of a table like this with a suspect sitting where I am now?* he recalled, finding this whole, current scenario ludicrous.

A moment later, the door opened and in strolled two men in suits. Scott immediately recognized the thickset, balding, older man. "Lt. Jetro?" he said, his eyes quizzical.

"So…we meet again, Mr. Arnold," Carter said, his eyes scorching Scott with their dark glare. The lieutenant slid out one of the chairs. It scratched along the tile floor as he sat down and worked it back up to the table.

The other man, a slender gentleman with a full head of ebony hair and dull grey eyes, approached Scott. "Mr. Arnold, I'm Lt. Pete McCoy. I'm a criminal investigator with the Pigeon Forge Police Department. Lt. Jetro and I would jest like to ask ya some quest'ns. I don't think it's neces'ary that ya remain handcuffed; do you?"

"I'd love to get these damn things off," Scott replied, bending forward.

Scott had been fighting a heightened sense of entrapment ever since the officer had handcuffed him at the motel. The only other time he had been fitted with handcuffs had been the night he had had two pairs snapped around his ankles, pinning him to the Nashville Railroad Bridge. Scott did not like any reminders of that night.

"Let's git ya out of these then," Pete graciously offered. He extracted a key from his pocket and proceeded to quickly unlock and remove Scott's handcuffs. He slipped the handcuffs and the key into the inside pocket of his suit jacket.

Scott brought his arms around in front of him and alternately rubbed one wrist and then the other. He realized that Lt. McCoy's helpful actions were an attempt to get him to relax and trust him. The detectives were hoping Scott would run off at the mouth and confess to being their killer. Scott now garnered that he must be a suspect in the death of Jameson Thornton as well; *otherwise, why would an investigator from Gatlinburg be here?*

Scott also knew, from watching the news, the district attorney in the area had been pushing hard for a conviction in the Jameson Thornton case, since it was so high profile. Scott guessed the Gatlinburg detective must be thrilled to have him in this interrogation room now as a suspect in a second, like M.O., murder. And making the detectives' cases even sweeter, Scott had just happened to be at the scene of both crimes.

Scott watched as Lt. McCoy walked around the table, pulled out the chair beside Lt. Jetro, sat down, and pulled his chair up to the table. Lt. McCoy's chair did not groan near as much as Lt. Jetro's had. Lt. Jetro had a lot more weight to push chair into tile.

"Well, we are all in our *comfy* chairs now," Scott stated, a hostile edge to his voice. "So why don't we get this over with?"

"That's a plan," Carter agreed, picking up his pen. He had laid a yellow legal pad on the table in front of him. Carter eyeballed Lt. McCoy, expecting him to take the lead, since they were seated in his interrogation room.

Pete folded his hands in front of him, glanced up and down, and took his time formulating his leadoff question. Scott tried not to fidget as he impatiently waited. Carter passed the time by scribbling an ink circle on his pad.

"Mr. Arnold, what exactly was yer relationship to our victim, Joe Butler?" Pete finally uttered, fanning a hand out toward him and meeting Scott's eyes.

"I didn't have a *relationship* with Joe Butler, per say," Scott answered, rubbing his chin and maintaining direct eye contact with Lt. McCoy. "I was hired as a private investigator by the victim's wife to prove he was being unfaithful. I've been following Joe to Adam Ridge Motel for the last few weeks. I have pictures of Joe meeting his young girlfriend there, him kissing her, and them fondling one another. I don't have any pictures of the two of them being intimate, because they always pulled the curtains shut. That was the first thing that alerted me that something was not right today. The curtains in the room were wide open."

"Is this the same PI case ya were workin' the mornin' you found Jameson Thornton dead in Gatlinburg?" Carter interjected his two cents, his black concentrated eyes tearing through Scott.

Scott broke eye contact with Lt. Jetro and looked down at the table. Reaching to rub his forehead, he chose his next words very carefully. Considering his current predicament, Scott wished he had never been less than truthful with this Gatlinburg investigator.

Scott finally raised his head, dared to meet the lieutenant's piercing gaze again, and confessed, "I…I wasn't really working a case that morning...at least not a PI case I was hired for."

"Hmm...go figure," Carter mocked, tapping his temple. His lips were pursed in a hard, disapproving line. "I knew there was more to the story than what ya were tellin' me, Mr. Arnold, and I knew we would meet again. And here we are. So why don't ya stop wastin' our time and jest come clean on what ya know."

"That's exactly what I intend to do," Scott told them both, his head bobbing up and down in agreement as he looked from Lt. Jetro to Lt. McCoy.

Pete sat up taller in his seat. His lackluster grey eyes seemed to perk up as he waited with eagerness to hear Scott's next words.

"I was in Gatlinburg the morning Jameson Thornton was murdered, because *someone* called my cell phone and alerted me Jameson had been murdered and the exact location where the murder had occurred," Scott revealed, looking from investigator to investigator.

Lt. McCoy's expression was unreadable, but Lt. Jetro clearly had a skeptical expression on his face. He shared his doubt with his next question to Scott. "Ya said *someone* called ya...I'm guessin' from this expression that ya did not recognize the caller's voice?"

"That's correct," Scott confirmed, nodding his head.

"But yet ya believed the caller's outlandish informat'n to be true? So much so that ya rushed off to Gatlinburg from Hendersonvill', TN. A what...three...four hour drive?" he probed, framing the side of his face with an L shape to his fingers.

"I did," Scott agreed, his head raising and lowering some more.

"Mind if I ask ya why?" Carter inquired, tapping two fingers from his other hand on the table.

"The killer also described the way in which Jameson Thornton had been murdered," Scott told them. "Of particular interest to me was the fact that his throat had been slit and his genitals mutilated. I knew then who I was talking to."

"And jest who might that have been?" the lieutenant asked, leaning forward a bit.

"A serial killer I've been tracking since my days on the LMPD Homicide Square. This man killed four people in Kentucky and four in Tennessee, most with the same exact M.O. – slit throat, mutilated genitals and handcuffed hands. Jameson Thornton and Joe Butler both had the same calling cards."

"So did ya git a tip about Joe Butler's murder today as well?" Pete finally chimed in after his long silence, folding his hands in front of him.

"In a roundabout way…yes, I did," Scott acknowledged, tapping a knuckle to his lip. "The same caller told me to show up at Adam Ridge Motel and go to Joe Butler's usual room. I was hoping upon hope that Joe had not been murdered. I feel responsible for Joe's death, because the only way the killer could have known about him was by following me around. I'm quite certain that the anonymous call you guys received about Joe's murder came from the killer as well. He knew I was in the room and set me up to take the fall."

Lt. Jetro and Lt. McCoy made brief eye contact. Scott Arnold certainly spun quite an elaborate story. They knew they needed to check on his facts.

"Look…I have a request to make of you guys," Scott said, interrupting the investigators' silent scrutiny.

"What's that?" Pete responded, looking back in Scott's direction.

"I need to call my wife. She needs to be put in the loop about all of this. This man I'm telling you about is very dangerous and devious. I thought he was just dangling a carrot in front of me with Jameson Thornton's murder…like…'ha, ha, I got away with it again. I'm right under your nose, but you still have no idea where I am'. But now, he has hit someone directly related to me. He tried once to kill me and failed, so maybe he is just trying to set me up for the murder instead. Regardless, I can't take the chance that he might still go after Sherri. My wife needs to know what has gone down here, so she can be watching her back more carefully."

"Why didn't ya tell *us*, and your wife, about this initially?" Carter asked, leaning back in his chair and tapping the butt of his pen against his notepad.

"Because I truly thought I could track this bastard down and turn him over to you guys before he killed again," Scott told them, looking from investigator to investigator. Neither one of them looked very impressed by this explanation.

Instead, Lt. Jetro shook a finger at Scott and threatened, "Ya know, at the very least, we could hold ya for obstruct'n." He was obviously aggravated and still doubtful about Scott's convoluted tale.

"If you decide to arrest me for obstruction, I would certainly understand," Scott told Carter, sounding repentant and looking down at the table. "My silence cost Joe his life," Scott berated himself. Looking back up at the detectives, Scott uttered, "Regardless of whatever you decide to do with me, you've got to catch this SOB before he hurts someone else. I'll be glad to share all the facts I have on this person with you. But you need to let me call my wife first."

The two detectives exchanged looks again. Finally, Lt. McCoy slid back his chair and stood. "I'll go git ya a phone," he told Scott.

"Thank you. I would appreciate that," Scott said, giving him a brief sign of a smile.

Scott was very worried for Sherri's safety now. He did not know if the investigators still intended to hold him or not, but regardless, Scott needed to warn Sherri that Jeanette was back on his murderous rampage again. Scott could not allow anything to happen to his wife.

"I need for ya to tell me everything ya know about this serial killer ya think we have on the loose," Lt. Jetro prodded, lifting his pen and legal pad from the table.

"There is no *think* about it," Scott clarified. "He *is* on the loose, and he will continue to kill unless he is caught and put away for life, or better yet…sentenced to death. So let's all work together to see that justice is done, okay?"

"Give me some relevant facts, Mr. Arnold, and I'll see what we can do," Carter proposed.

"Okay," Scott agreed. Relaxing a bit for the first time since being hauled in by the police, he rested his back against his chair. Tapping his fingers together in front of him, Scott began, "Bizarre as this may sound, our killer is a man in a woman's body. His last known identity was Debbie Gray, a name – and identity – he stole from one of his victims in Kentucky. Does that give you some clue as to what kind of a sick bastard we are dealing with?" Scott asked.

Carter looked up from his notepad and merely bobbled his head up and down.

Scott continued, "I can guarantee you that he has changed identities – and most likely his appearance – again. When last seen, he was a large breasted woman with medium-length, dark black hair and green eyes and weighed about 175 pounds. He/she was working as a security guard at the Gaylord Entertainment Center in Nashville, TN. While living, and working, in the Nashville area, he also managed to brutally kill four people…and cause the death of a fifth person. As I mentioned before, these murders all had the same M.O. as the crimes in this area: Sliced throat; handcuffed victims; and knife to the family jewels. These four victims were in addition to the four people killed in Kentucky; all but one of the Kentucky victims was the same M.O. as well."

As Scott paused to take a breath, Lt. McCoy opened the door and joined them in the room again. He held a telephone in his hands. He sat it on the table in front of Scott, and proceeded to plug the phone cord into a phone jack on the wall. "Make your call," he directed Scott, sliding out the chair beside Lt. Jetro and having a seat once again.

"Thanks," Scott said, flashing him a smile of gratitude. He wasted no time whipping up the receiver and dialing Sherri's work number.

"Sergeant Arnold," Sherri's voice said a moment later.

Scott fought the urge to smile. He never tired of hearing Sherri use his last name as her own. He loved knowing she was his wife.

"Sherri, it's…uh…Scott. I…er…I have a problem," he hesitantly revealed, glancing at the detectives. They were watching him carefully, and Scott knew they were listening to his every word.

"What's wrong?" Sherri asked, on alert. Scott was usually jovial when he called her, but now, he sounded much too somber.

"Let's just say Jeanette is at it again…" he divulged, running his hand up and down the telephone cord.

"Shit!" Sherri snapped, interrupting. She sat up straight in her seat and squeezed the telephone against her ear now. "What's that mean? Are ya alright?"

"I...I'm fine," Scott was quick to assure her, even though Carter's intense, too dark eyes were making his skin crawl. "But a man I was investigating for infidelity was murdered today. His throat was slashed; his hands were handcuffed; and there was a knife left in his testicles."

"Crap! So that means Jeanette is followin' ya," Sherri logically concluded. Her back had tensed against her chair and she tapped a fisted hand on her armrest. "Where are ya?"

"I'm at the Pigeon Forge Police Station," Scott told her. "I'm safe," he said, glancing at the detectives again. Then he told her with concern, "You're the one who needs to watch your back. Jeanette is playing with me," he revealed. Then pausing, looking down at the tabletop, and making a circle with his index finger, he slowly added, "In fact...the police arrested me as a suspect...."

"They what?!" Sherri asked, leaving the phone receiver propped between her neck and ear and flailing her hands out in front of her. "Why would they do somethin' like that?"

"They got an anonymous tip about the murder, and when they showed up, I was there in the bathroom with the dead body. I was in the room because I also got an anonymous tip to be there," Scott informed her, pinching his lips together, rolling his eyes, and shaking his head at his stupidity.

"So ya're tellin' me Jeanette set ya up," Sherri put two and two together. She was rubbing her temple now.

"Yes...actually...*twice*," Scott slowly disclosed, exhaling.

"Twice?" Sherri questioned, her eyes narrowing.

"I was called to the murder site of Jameson Thornton as well," he revealed, sliding his hand back and forth across the table's edge.

"You were...what?!" Sherri barked, clutching the phone receiver in her hand again. "So that means ya think Jeanette killed Jameson too. Why are ya jest now tellin' me this, Scott? Jameson Thornton's murder was several weeks ago. We watched reports of his murder together on television."

"I know we did," Scott agreed, moving his head up and down in concurrence. "I should have said something to you, but I thought I could handle it on my own..."

"Shit!" Sherri cursed again. "So *now* exactly what do ya want me to do?" she asked, breathing fire.

"I want you to be extra careful. I don't know what Jeanette's next move might be. I'm worried about you, and I'm worried about Angela. If Jeanette's only motive was to set me up, he's accomplished that. But I'm scared he might try and kill someone else close to me, and he could target you or Angela. The best place for me is in jail here in Pigeon Forge. If he thinks I'm being charged for the murders, then he might back off from doing any further killing. And chances are Jeanette was watching the hotel and saw the police haul me out of Joe's room in handcuffs."

"Scott, is there a detective there with ya?" Sherri asked, sounding very no-nonsense.

"There are two of them here," Scott replied, looking up at the faces of Lt. Jetro and McCoy for the first time in several moments. He continued, "One detective is from Gatlinburg, where Jameson was murdered, and the other is from here in Pigeon Forge, where the other murder occurred."

"Okay. Lit me talk to the Pigeon Forge detective, please," she requested, sounding very formal.

"Alright. I love you. Stay safe," Scott said.

"I love ya too," Sherri said, but her words sounded forced.

Scott knew Sherri was furious with him for having not shared all he knew about the murder of Jameson Thornton. He quickly handed the phone receiver to Lt. McCoy. "My wife would like to have a word with you," Scott told him, looking sheepish.

Lt. McCoy's face scrunched, but he took the phone from Scott. "Lt. Pete McCoy," he identified himself; then asked, "What can I do for ya today?"

"Lt. McCoy, this is Sergeant Arnold with the Hendersonvill' Police Department," she wasted no time identifying herself.

"Yes, ma'am," he said, showing respect for a fellow law enforcement official.

"I understand that my husband, Scott Arnold, was arrested on suspicion of murder."

"Yes, ma'am," Lt. McCoy responded again.

"Do you intend to hold him?"

"We're not certain," he honestly shared, flashing a look at Scott. "We were in the process of questionin' him when he expressed a valid concern for yer safety, so we allowed him to make a call to you. But we need to interrogate him more. He has raised several compellin' quest'ns in our minds, which we need to follow up on. I will tell ya that, for now, circumstantially, he is still considered a very strong suspect in the two murder cases."

"I have input on murders that occurred in the Nashvill' area that might shed some light on yer current cases," Sherri shared, tapping a finger on her desk.

"We'd certainly be more than happy to have any informat'n ya can share, Sergeant," Pete told her.

"I'm goin' to come to Pigeon Forge to meet with ya'll. Can ya'll hold Mr. Arnold there until I arrive?" she requested. "I think he would be safer at the police department than anywhere else right now. And right now, his confinement might lend a hand in my safety as well."

"We could certainly do that," Pete readily agreed, looking over at Scott again. He was in no hurry to release Mr. Arnold. Until they learned otherwise, Scott was still their prime suspect and considered a very dangerous individual.

"I'll be there as soon as possible," Sherri told him.

"We look forward to meetin' you, Sergeant Arnold," Lt. McCoy encouraged, anxious for whatever light Sherri could shed on their current maze of murders.

Before Pete had a chance to say goodbye, Scott waved a hand and interjected, "Lt. McCoy, could I please speak to my wife again?"

"Sergeant Arnold, yer husband wants to talk to ya again," Pete told her, his eyes shifting from Scott's face sideways to the phone receiver.

He was about to hand the phone over to Scott, but Sherri stopped him, saying, "Tell Mr. Arnold I'll talk to him when I git to Pigeon Forge. Thank ya'll for all your help in this matter, Lieutenant. Goodbye."

"Goodbye," he barely got a chance to say before he heard her hang up. Placing the phone back on its base, Pete reiterated Sherri's message to Scott, "She said she'll talk to ya when she gits here."

"Damn!" Scott cursed under his breath, rapping a fist on the table in front of him.

Scott did not want Sherri anywhere near him. He wanted her to stay put in Hendersonville and keep an eye out on herself and Angela. But he knew well how headstrong his wife could be, so he realized there was nothing he could do to stop Sherri from coming to Pigeon Forge.

"Can we git back to what ya were tellin' me about our killer?" Lt. Jetro asked, changing gears. He would deal with Scott Arnold's wife when she arrived. Right now, he wanted to continue gathering facts on the killer Scott claimed they had on the loose in their area. "I take it, from the bits and pieces of the conversat'n I heard with yer wife, that another name the killer goes by is Jeanette?"

"Yeah, that's right," Scott confirmed. He began to fill in other details on the murderous rampage of Jeanette 'O'Riley' Peterson a.k.a. Debbie Gray. Scott realized he had over three hours to kill before Sherri would appear on the scene, and he wanted to use some of this time to fill the detectives in on as many facts about Jeanette as he could.

Chapter 11

Part of the Team

After Scott finished giving his statement to the detectives, he was surprised to learn that he was being sent to the Sevier County Jail in Sevierville, Tennessee. Sevierville was right up the road from Pigeon Forge, and their jail served as a holding facility for Pigeon Forge criminals as well as those in Sevierville. When Scott arrived at the jail, he found he was not booked on any charges. Instead, a corrections officer just shuffled him off to a private cell, locked the door, and left him there in solitude.

Scott sat on a small bunk in the room, staring at bleak concrete walls and metal bars and trying to ignore the obnoxious odor coming from a filthy toilet a few feet over from him. Scott did not understand why they were holding him without booking him for a crime. He assumed the detectives must have valid reasons. He hoped to find out soon what that reason could be. Scott glanced at his watch over and over, anxious for Sherri to make her appearance and spring him from this hellhole and possibly shed some light on his incarceration. Scott was certain Lt. McCoy would tell Sherri where he was.

Sherri finally arrived, but not before Scott had had to spend several exasperating hours in the cramped, foul-smelling cell. He was lying on a bunk with his eyes closed, trying to tune everything out and feel less claustrophobic, when the much desired jingle-jangle of keys in the lock of his jail door met Scott's ears. Scott bolted to a sitting position and stared with relief as the jailor swung his door open.

"Ya have a visitor, Mr. Arnold," a plump woman in a corrections uniform barked at him. She had fire engine red hair that was pulled back in a bun so tight that it seemed to have pulled her cheeks and eyes back with it.

Scott looked past this harsh looking woman to catch a glimpse of his stunning, impeccable wife. As usual, Sherri was dressed in a curve-flattering woman's blouse and pantsuit; her brown hair shone and was styled in a manner attractive to her healthy, glowing face; and she wore just the right amount of eye makeup to bring out the warm glow in her chocolate eyes. Scott was always glad to see his wife, but he was exceedingly grateful to see her today.

He stood and took long strides toward the opened cell door with a relieved smile spreading across his face. He hoped his time here would be short now. If Scott had not known it before, he was certain now that he was not cut out to be a prisoner.

Scott felt an enormous wave of relief as Sherri stepped through the opened door of his cell and he instantly engulfed her in a tight hug. "Man, it's good to see you!" he gushed, kissing the side of her soft mouth and inhaling her intoxicating perfume. As Scott pulled back, however, he discovered that Sherri was not smiling and did not seem as delighted to see him.

"Scott, we need to talk," Sherri told him, her eyes all seriousness.

"What's wrong?" he asked, distressed.

Sherri seemed to ignore Scott's question. Instead, she turned her attention to the nearby corrections officer. "Is there someplace private where me and my husband can go ta talk?" Sherri asked this woman.

"Sure," she replied.

"Does that mean I'm free to go?" Scott asked, looking over at the corrections officer as well.

"No official charges have been filed against you, so you are free to go," the woman told him. There was no sign of a smile on her face, only a hard frown.

Regardless, Scott flashed this woman a smile. He quickly stepped out of the jail cell, not wishing to give anyone a chance to change their mind about his release. Scott actually wanted to bolt out of the entire building, but he forced himself to stay put in the dim corridor.

Sherri also stepped out of the cell and came to a halt beside Scott. "Can ya take us to that private place now, so we can talk?" she asked the corrections officer.

"Follow me. I'll take you there," this woman said and started away.

Sherri fell into pace behind this robust woman and Scott followed at Sherri's heel. He was anxious to get to a private spot, so he could hear whatever Sherri needed to say to him.

A few moments later, they came to a small meeting room. The corrections officer reached in and flipped a switch. Fluorescent lights flickered and then lit the room bright. "You'll have all the privacy you need here," she told Sherri, stepping aside. "Just turn off the lights and shut the door when you are through."

"Thanks. Will do," Sherri assured her. As the corrections officer turned and hurried away up the hallway, Sherri walked through the door into the conference room.

Scott followed, pulling the door closed behind him. He watched as Sherri settled herself in at the head of the table. He took a seat to her right, occupying one of the other five, vacant chairs. "So what do we need to talk about? Is something wrong?" Scott asked, looking concerned.

"I cain't believe ya would even have the gall to ask me that," Sherri stated in a growl. Her narrowed, darkened eyes pierced Scott's.

She's furious with me, Scott was quick to conclude. "I guess you're angry with me for not telling you about the tip I got about Jameson Thornton's murder," Scott commented, glancing down at the shiny conference table in front of him.

"Gee...were ya always this bright, or were ya just bowled over by some great revela'n?" Sherri sarcastically questioned. Her eyes were still shooting arrows.

"Sherri, you have every reason to be mad at me...." Scott agreed, holding up his hands and looking like a whipped dog.

"Why don't ya tell me somethin' I don't already know?" she challenged, grinding her teeth. Sherri's hands were flat on the table and she was tapping her index fingers. "Scott, I don't do well at all with secrets from the man I love," she told him, sounding more hurt than angry for the first time. "My daddy always told me that if a man will lie about one thing...he'll lie about most anythin'. If ya mess with the trust in our relat'nship and destroy that, ya'll eventually destroy everythang we have. Do ya understand that?"

"That would be the last thing I would ever want to do," Scott told her, looking contrite. He cautiously reached to rub one of Sherri's hands. "I love you, Sherri, from the bottom of my heart," he said, touching his other hand to his chest. "I just can't stand the thought of anything happening to you. I only wanted to protect you...."

"I don't need any macho man stunts from you, Scott," Sherri interjected, bristling again. She pulled her hand away from his touch. "I'm a police sergeant. I can take care of myself," she pointed out, sitting tall in her chair.

"Sherri, I'm not trying to reduce you to some wimpy damsel-in-distress," Scott tried to assure her, fingering his wedding band. Looking her back in the eye, he added, "But you have to understand that it still haunts me that you almost died on the Nashville Railroad Bridge not long ago because of me. I can't take a chance of that happening again...."

"An excellent point!" Sherri praised, slapping the table with one hand. "We would not have been on the Nashvill' Railroad Bridge, at the brink of death, if ya hadn't of tried to play the Lone Ranger and capture Jeanette by yerself. If ya don't want to take a chance of puttin' me in harm's way again, then ya'll keep me in the loop. Workin' together as a team, I think we have an excellent chance of finally capturin' Jeanette and puttin' her away for good. Then she cain't hurt me, you, or anyone else. But if ya go out on a limb by yerself, ya could not only put yerself in harm's way, but a lot of innocent people."

Sherri's wise words struck home with Scott. After a few, long, pensive moments, with a saddened expression, he admitted, "You're right. As much as I don't want you involved in all this, Sherri, you already are. And I feel like I've screwed up again and cost Joe Butler his life this time. I wish I had told not only you, but Lt. Jetro, about who I knew the killer to be. I don't know if he could have stopped Jeanette from killing Joe…but now, I'll always wonder if it would have made a difference. You're married to a real screw-up, do you know that?" Scott asked, looking miserable and squirming in his seat.

Sherri's anger with Scott dissipated just as quickly as it had arisen. "Ya're not a screw-up, Scott," she said, reaching to clasp his hand this time. "You did what ya thought was best, because ya badly wanted to git a killer off of the streets once and for all. And I, of all people, know how easily Jeanette spooks and how quickly she can pack up and move on. I want her off the streets as badly as ya do, and so do Lt. Jetro and Lt. McCoy."

"I don't doubt *your* passion about getting Jeanette off the streets, Sherri," Scott told her, his eyes locking with hers. "But I'm not so sure about Lt. Jetro and McCoy. I think Lt. Jetro still suspects *I* might be the serial killer. And I can certainly understand why, considering I was at both crimes scenes. And when you get right down to it, I've been involved with all the other murders as well."

"Yeah, I know," Sherri agreed, nodding. "But the sticker is…it wasn't yer DNA at the crime scenes in Kentucky," she said pointing at him. She took a quick breath and then continued, "It was Jeanette's DNA at those crimes scenes. And even though we found no good DNA evidence at the crime locations in Tennessee, the crimes had the same exact M.O. And who did we find nearby…good ol' Debbie Gray, whose DNA, of course, matched to Jeanette Peterson. I pointed out to Lt. Jetro and Lt. McCoy that we have a much more solid case against Jeanette Peterson than they do against you. You and I, and these detectives, all know that DNA evidence doesn't lie."

"I hope so, Sherri," Scott said, looking skeptical. Then exhaling, he added, "Because Jeanette is big time playing games this time around. Not only did he set me up to look like the killer at these last two crimes, but he left me a little memento to prove it was him."

"What kind of memento?" Sherri questioned, her eyes narrowing as she stared Scott in the eye.

"We didn't go to L.A. just for our honeymoon," Scott said in a quiet voice, breaking eye contact and looking down at the table.

"I already know that, Scott," Sherri reminded him. She added, "When I found the tickets, ya said ya already had to go there to do some P.I. work."

"Right," Scott agreed, meeting Sherri's eyes again. Biting his thumbnail, Scott put in, "I need to come clean with you about everything now, Sherri. And part of all that's gone down with Jeanette lately has to do with L.A."

"What happened in L.A., Scott?" Sherri asked, sitting up tall in her chair. Her eyes were fixated on his.

"I found *this* laying on top of Jameson's hands," Scott replied, pulling his hand from his pant's pocket and laying his University of Louisville Cardinal keychain with his van key attached on the table in front of Sherri.

"The key to your van," Sherri said, glancing with surprise from the keychain and key to Scott's face again. "That disappeared when Jeanette kidnapped ya. He ditched yer van at a nearby Wal-Mart. But neither yer keychain or yer key was in it," Sherri spoke from recall.

"That's what I mean about Jeanette leaving me a memento. He sent me a copy of a typewritten note, which I would guess was part of an e-mail. The note told when and where Jameson Thornton's body was being laid out. Along with this item was a handwritten note that told me it would be to my advantage to go to Beverly Hills and pay my final respects to Jameson Thornton."

"God, Scott, you could have been walkin' into a deadly trap. Do ya realize that?" Sherri asked with both concern and aggravation, shaking her head.

"I had my gun with me, Sherri. I didn't go to the park empty-handed," he told her, sounding confident in his safety.

"Jeanette could have been set up somewheres close with a sniper rifle and took ya out before ya knew what hit ya," Sherri postulated, a cold chill running up and down her spine.

"I suppose. But, as you know, that's not really Jeanette's style, Sherri. I do believe he was in that park somewhere that day, blending in with the crowd. It's hard telling what he even looks like now."

"I jest cain't believe ya've gone off on yer own and done all these crazy things, Scott," Sherri growled, squeezing her cheeks between her hands. "Is there anything else ya're keepin' from me? Because now is the time to come clean. I won't stand for you hidin' things from me any longer. Is that understood, Scott?" Sherri stated her ultimatum, a spark of anger in her eyes again.

"That's understood loud and clear, Sherri," Scott assured her, his head bobbing up and down. He also gave her hand another affirming squeeze. "I've laid all my cards on the table. I swear that I'm not holding anything else back from you, Sherri. You know everything I know now."

"I better," she stated, giving him a hard stare. "Because I expect us *all* to get our heads around this now and work together. Are we agreed?" she asked, her eyes meeting his again.

"Yes," Scott reluctantly agreed, mashing his lips together. He did not want Sherri involved, but he knew he had no choice. He would just have to take extra care to watch over her until they managed to catch Jeanette and put him away once and for all.

"Good," Sherri said, giving Scott a forced smile and patting his hand. Sliding her chair back from the table and standing, she surprised Scott by saying, "Let's go home, Mr. Arnold."

"Do you mean it?" Scott asked, looking up at Sherri and sounding chipper for the first time in several moments.

"Yeah," Sherri said. "I think ya've been punished enough for one day. I had somethin' to do with the jail thang," she said, averting her eyes. "I called Lt. McCoy back and asked them to hold ya *in jail* and…short of putting ya in with a bunch of thugs…to make it as uncomfortable as possible. I wanted ya to learn yer lesson for lyin' to me. Plus…I was afraid if they let ya out, ya might go snoopin' around where yer butt didn't belong again.

"Guess I deserved that," Scott agreed, looking repentant as he also slid his chair back and stood.

In actuality, Scott could not wait to get out of this building. He did not care if he ever saw the inside of a jail cell, or even the inside of this jailing facility, again. As he and Sherri made their way out of the room, Scott's heart was warmed when Sherri draped an arm around his side and pulled up tight to him. "Just remember that from now on, we are a team in *everythang*," she reminded him, her eyes intense. "And as a team, we can accomplish anythang. Ya got that?"

"Got it loud and clear, Mrs. Arnold," Scott replied. He bent to seal his words with a kiss, happy that Sherri's anger with him was finally dissipating once and for all.

They quickly made their way along sparsely lighted hallways to the front door of the building and to Sherri's car. As she started the car, a thought occurred to Scott, so he asked, "Um…is my van still at the motel?"

"I imagine it is," Sherri replied.

"Well…why don't we leave it there for now?" he suggested.

"Don't feel like drivin' home?" Sherri asked, glancing at him with concern.

"Don't feel like being parted from you again so soon," Scott replied, reaching to cup her closest hand, which had been resting on the seat beside her. Scott also flashed her a bittersweet smile.

"Well...I've certainly missed yer sweet talk. That's fer sure," Sherri said returning his smile. Her eyes also sparkled as their eyes met and held. "We'll drive on over ta the motel and let them know yer van is there, so they don't have it towed. Then we'll head on home. I'll drive ya back tomorrow mornin' to pick up yer van. I want to talk to Lt. Jetro some more face to face anyway."

"Maybe we *both* should talk to Lt. Jetro some more tomorrow," Scott suggested.

"No," Sherri vetoed, shaking her head. "Jest me," she said, touching her chest with her hand. She went on to explain, "I want to talk to him one police detective to another. As far as I know, ya're still a suspect. So I want ya to keep yer distance."

"I guess that might not be such a bad idea," Scott agreed with a frustrated frown. He still could not believe he had allowed Jeanette to set him up like he had. Scott knew he was smarter than that.

"Give me directions to the motel," Sherri said, putting the car in reverse and backing out of her parking space.

Scott instructed Sherri on which direction to go, even though he was not looking forward to going back to the motel – the scene of Joe's murder. But Scott realized what Sherri was proposing would be wise. They did not want to have to mess with getting his van from some impound lot if they could avoid it. Regardless, Scott knew he would just be glad when they left the motel and headed to the only place he wanted to be right now...home.

Chapter 12

Piecing it all Together

The next afternoon, Sherri showed up at the Gatlinburg Police Department to meet with Lt. Jetro again. Settled in a chair in his office, Sherri wasted no time inquiring, "So what have you and Lt. McCoy garnered, thus far, from the informat'n ya've pulled together for yer murder investigat'ns."

There was a long pause and then with a grave expression on his face, the lieutenant told her, "Sherri, I have to be honest with ya. Of all the evidence we've gathered thus far, we could jest as easily build a strong case against yer husband as we could against...this Jeanette...uh Debbie Gray ...uh whatever name this other individual is currently goin' by."

"How do ya figure?" Sherri questioned, looking exasperated. She squeezed the arms of her chair to release some of the nervous irritation now eating at her gut. She was beginning to think she had chosen to meet with the wrong detective. She had chosen Lt. Jetro, versus Lt. McCoy, because Carter was the older, and more seasoned, detective. Carter had revealed the day before that he was forty eight years old and had been a detective for over fifteen years. Lines on Carter's face, bald spots showing on his scalp, and the sedantary bulge in his stomach also attested to his long service.

Carter hated seeing the look of irritation on Sherri's pretty, fresh, young face. Attractively dressed in a lady's pantsuit, she brought a scent of fresh air to his office. But,

Carter knew he needed to stick to business and the facts, so he continued, "Scott has had some connect'n to *all* of these murders, Sherri. *Each*, and *every* one…" he pointed out, tapping the side of his hand against his desk to add extra emphasis to the words he considered most important.

"Yeah," Sherri agreed, nodding. Then she quickly added, "He was involved in the first four murders in Kentucky as the investigatin' detective…."

"One of those victims, I've learned, was a girlfriend of Scott's. And I've also uncovered that Mr. Arnold was found kneelin' in her blood at the murder site," the lieutenant relayed, thumbing through his notes.

"I'm impressed by the amount of informat'n ya've uncovered in such a short time, Carter," Sherri commented, forcing an appreciative smile.

"Well, I have to be honest with ya, Sherri. I started gatherin' informat'n on Scott after I discovered him at the Jameson Thornton murder site. He was our one, and *only*, suspect. And his story about jest happenin' upon the body jest did not rang true. And as it turns out, his story was *not* true. Once I've been lied to about one thang, it makes me wonder how many other thangs Scott might be lyin' about," Carter told her, his intimidating dark eyes all seriousness and his mouth taunt.

"I can certainly understand that," Sherri agreed, bobbling her head again. "And ya're right about Scott and his girlfriend, Debbie. Scott *was* found at Debbie's place of death…and he *was* kneelin' in her blood when he was discovered," Sherri fully disclosed, leaning back in her chair. "But the most important fact that ya need to take into account is that Scott was cleared by LMPD's Public Integrity Unit of any wrongdoing in that crime. Didn't ya also receive this informat'n?"

"I did," Lt. Jetro was quick to concede, bobbing his head. Rocking back in his desk chair, he paused, exhaled, and rebuked, "But, quite frankly, when it comes to big city police departments and their investigat'ns of one of their own, I'm not always real confident in their findin's. Seems they always seem to find in favor of their fellow officer…no matter what. Know what I'm sayin'?"

"Yeah, I know there is a lot more corrupt'n in big city police departments than in smaller one like yours…and even ours," Sherri conceded, steepling her fingers and touching her nails to her chin. "But you need to remember the bottom line of all this, Carter," she reminded him. "And that bottom line is…there was DNA evidence found that directly links Jeanette to the murders and *not* Scott. How did Jeanette's hairs and bodily fluids git at two of the murder locations if he wasn't involved? And Jeanette is also linked to each of the people who were murdered…much closer than Scott. Renee Peterson, Jeanette's first victim, was his office assistant; Chad Kennison, the second victim, was servin' jury duty and Jeanette was one of the jury administrators; Debbie Gray, Scott's girlfriend, had also been serving on jury duty…and while we're talking about Debbie, let's not forget that Jeanette stole Debbie's identity when he fled Louisville and moved to Nashville. Which brangs me to a whole 'nother point…why would an innocent person flee a city anyway?"

"Good question!" Lt. Jetro commented, slapping the corner of his desk. Then he asked, "What if Jeanette was fleeing Scott? Many people fearing for their lives change identities, and Jeanette, knowing Debbie Gray was dead, might have found Debbie's identity the most logical to steal. Scott would never think to search for his dead girlfriend; would he?"

"Oh…Jeanette was fleeing Scott alright," Sherri agreed, raising her voice an octave and sitting up tall in her chair. Lowering her voice again, she continued her argument with Lt. Jetro. "I can assure you, Lieutenant, that Jeanette did not flee Scott because he feared for his life. Jeanette ran because he realized Scott and the LMPD were closing in on prosecuting him for the murders...."

"That's not what I've learned," the lieutenant contradicted, emphatically shaking his head. "My research showed that a young lady by the name of Stacy Prescott was arrested for Chad Kennison's murder, and was the prime suspect in the other murders ya've mentioned as well. In fact, they briefly put her on trial for Chad's murder, but the charges were dropped after the DNA evidence *Scott* discovered gave them reasonable doubt in proceeding with her prosecution. Isn't it amazin' that Scott came up with this informat'n, pointin' a solid finger at Jeanette Peterson, single-handedly?"

"Well...yeah! Scott's an amazin' detective," Sherri defended and praised all in the same breath, flinging a hand out to the side. She fought not to circle her hands, indicating that she would like to strangle Carter. Instead, Sherri hurried on with her crucial argument of Scott's innocence, "While we are on the subject of Stacy Prescott, another great point is...since Stacy was already standin' trial for one of the murders and suspected for all the others, why wouldn't Scott have just allowed Stacy to take the fall if Scott was the guilty party? Why set up Jeanette? That is what ya're inferrin' aren't ya, Lt. Jetro?" Sherri questioned.

"That's exactly what I'm suggestin', yeah." Carter owned up to, raising and lowering his head a few times. "And I'll give you a reason why I think Scott decided to point the finger at Jeanette instead of leavin' it with Stacy," he said, tapping a pen on a stack of papers on his desk. "As you've already mentioned, Jeanette had some connection to *all* the victims, unlike Stacy. I think the LMPD might have been able to build a case against Stacy for her boyfriend Chad's murder. But I don't think they could have pinned the other murders on her, so that might have left the other murders still open to investigat'n, and maybe Mr. Arnold wanted to insure that they all went away. What better way to do that than linkin' them all to one person?"

"You really believe this ludicrous scenario, don't ya?" Sherri asked, concerned for the first time. She rubbed her forehead as a headache began to take shape. "Ya still haven't explained how Jeanette's DNA…her hair and bodily fluids …was found at crime scenes?"

"I don't know exactly how this…Jeanette person's …hairs and bodily fluids got at the crimes scenes. And quite frankly, Sherri, neither do you. All we know for certain is that hairs and bodily fluids matchin' Jeanette's DNA were found at two…jest *two*, mind ya…murder locations," he pointed out, holding up two fingers. "And as ya already mentioned, Jeanette knew both the victims: Chad Kennison, she could have met through jury duty and Mitchell Peterson was her husband. Both men likely had an intimate encounter with Jeanette that left behind Jeanette's DNA at the murder sites. But did Jeanette kill both these men after these encounters? We don't know. I talked to Roger Matthews, Scott's ex-partner from the LMPD, and he even admitted to havin' serious doubts about Jeanette Peterson as the murderer at first."

"Yeah…at *first!*" Sherri agreed, flailing both hands in front of her to emphasize her point again. "That was before Scott brought him evidence…*true blue* evidence…mind ya! And that evidence was DNA linked to the crimes scenes… This evidence was strong enough to change Roger Matthew's mind. And from what I gather from Scott, Roger's mind was not easily changed. And there are also a few other *pertinent facts* I need to point out to ya, Lieutenant," Sherri paused, drawing a shallow breath. "One…a size eight, uniform shoe print was taken from my Hendersonvill' crime scene. Scott's more like a size ten. And guess what size Jeanette happens to wear? And since, as Debbie Gray, Jeanette was workin' as a security guard for the Gaylord in Nashvill', he jest happened to be wearin' uniform shoes each day." Pausing for only a second more, she hurried on, "And let's not forget that on the day I was supposed to arrest Jeanette for our Hendersonvill' murder as well as the other murders in the Nashvill' area, Jeanette knocked Scott unconscious and took him hostage. Then she left him for dead handcuffed to the Nashville Railroad Bridge…."

"Whoa!" Carter stopped her, automatically throwing his hands up palm out. "Lit's git our facts straight here, shall we, Sherri?"

"What's that mean? Those are the facts," Sherri argued, leaning forward in her chair and grasping her hands together.

"Not exactly," Carter argued, rubbing his own hands together. "I also talked to Lt. Gregory in Nashvill', and after he got done tellin' me that he *also* initially suspected Scott of the murders in the Nashville area, he went on to tell me about Scott's attempted murder on the Nashville Railroad Bridge. Accordin' to Lt. Gregory's account, it was that a psychiatrist by the name of Wallace Cleaver that brought Scott to the bridge, beat the hell out of him, and then handcuffed him to the bridge. Then before the train actually struck Scott, the doctor seemed to have a change of heart and helped you to free Scott. Then the psychiatrist was tragically struck by the train and thrown into the river. Lt. Gregory still is not sure what to make of the doctor's involvement in Scott's kidnapping. And since the doctor is no longer around to question, I guess we'll never truly know why he was involved. But my point is…it was

Wallace Cleaver who left Scott for dead...not this Jeanette person."

"I can guarantee ya that Dr. Cleaver was actin' on orders from Jeanette," Sherri argued, exhaling with frustration.

"No, actually ya cain't guarantee me that, Sherri," Carter maintained, leaning back in his chair and crossing his arms. "Ya have no more idea what Wallace Cleaver's motive was than anyone else involved in this investigat'n. As I understand it, Dr. Cleaver was this Jeanette's, or Debbie Gray's, psychiatrist. Maybe she told him she was being threatened by Scott, and he decided to take matters into his own hands when he found out his client had taken Scott hostage. We don't know. All we can do is conjecture at this point...."

"Which is all ya've been doin' all along," Sherri insisted. "What, besides conjecture and circumstantial evidence, do you have linkin' Scott to the murders? The way I see it, you don't have one shred of physical evidence against Scott, Lieutenant. Come on, Carter, let's get real here! Jeanette is our most worthy murder suspect, and ya know it! We need to be trackin' Jeanette down and be chargin' him as a serial killer in two states," Sherri earnestly made a case, wringing her hands.

"I certainly agree that we need to track Jeanette down, Sherri. We need answers from him to a lot of open-ended questions. If he can't provide some logical reason why his DNA might have shown up at the crime scenes, then I agree...he is most likely our killer. But if he provides a feasible reason why his hairs and bodily fluids might have been found there, it's a whole 'nother ballgame. Scott was the one who 'showed up' at both Jameson Thornton's murder site and Joe Butler's. And Scott has the link to Joe Butler; and it's

Scott fingerprints at Joe's murder site, not this Jeanette person."

"Yeah, but I need to enlighten you on two other important items, Lieutenant," Sherri told him, extracting her purse from the floor, sitting it in her lap and unzipping it. "First," she said, holding up a finger. "Scott and I went to L.A. at the time Jameson Thornton was laid out for viewin'. Scott went there because he received these two notes in the mail," she said. She reached inside her purse and pulled forth the typewritten note telling where Jameson Thornton would be laid out and the handwritten note requesting Scott come to L.A. to view Jameson's body. Leaning forward, she handed these items across the desk to Carter. Sherri gave Carter a few moments to read the items. When he looked back up at her with curious eyes, she continued. "When Scott went up to view Jameson's body, he found this item layin' by Jameson's folded hands." Sherri pulled Scott's U of L Cardinal keychain and key from her purse. She again leaned forward and handed this item to Carter. "That's Scott's keychain and key to his van. These items *both* went missin' after Scott was kidnapped by Jeanette. Jeanette ditched Scott's van at a local Wal-Mart, but Jeanette did not leave Scott's key and keychain in the van. Jeanette kept these items. Isn't it curious that these items turned up on Jameson Thornton's dead body in L.A.?" Sherri asked, briefly pausing. A slight smile played at the corners of her mouth. She was pleased with the information she had just imparted to Lieutenant Jetro.

"And you personally saw Scott take these items from Jameson Thornton's body in L.A.?" Carter questioned, skeptical.

"No," Sherri was slow to admit, breaking eye contact with Carter for the first time in several moments. "Scott just gave me the keychain and key yesterday when he was coming clean about all that had gone down with him and Jeanette as of late."

"I see," Carter commented, nodding and interlacing his fingers in front of him.

"This keychain and chain *were* taken by Jeanette," Sherry staunchly maintained, giving Carter a determined, concentrated stare. "Scott hasn't had them hidden away somewhere and just produced them yesterday," she said, guessing what Carter was thinking.

"I didn't say that, Sherri," Carter pointed out. "If this note is authentic…," he said, holding the handwritten note up in the air. "Then someone wanted Scott to go to L.A. to Jameson Thornton's viewing for some reason," he stated.

"Oh…that note is *definitely* authentic," Sherri insisted. "And I can prove it…"

"How's that?" Carter asked, his eyes doubtful.

Sherri pulled forth one other item from her purse and handed it to Carter. "This is a note Scott wrote me a week ago. Ya're more than welcome to have a handwritin' specialist compare the two notes. I'm certain they will confirm that two different people wrote them. And I'll do you one better…when you bring Jeanette in for questionin', you need to get another sample of his handwritin'. I'm willin' to bet that the sample you gather will match to that note."

Carter was still looking down at the two notes he had laid on his desk. He had to admit that there was a drastic difference in the two writing styles. He would, however, have a handwriting specialist give their educated opinion.

"So what was the other important item you wanted to enlighten me on, Sherri," Carter asked, changing the subject. He looked back up and met her eyes again.

"Jest that I called Scott's cell phone company and had them pull records of his last few weeks' incomin' calls," she told him. Tapping her fingers together, she continued, "While they unfortunately could *not* track the exact location, they could tell me that two calls came in from your area; one the morning Jameson Thornton was murdered, and another the day Joe Butler was murdered. This substantiates Scott's story that he received anonymous calls about both murders."

"It shows that he got calls from this area, but it doesn't tell us who made those calls," Lt. Jetro disputed. "Since Scott was workin' a PI case in the area, those calls could have come from Joe Butler's wife, checkin' up on her case."

"You're damned and determined to pin these murders on Scott, aren't you, Lieutenant?" Sherri freely accused, her pinched face clearly showing her aggravation.

"I'm not determined to *pin* these murders on anyone, Sherri," he assured her, leaning back and swiveling his chair. "I'm only tryin' to make sure I have all the facts. I want to make sure the right person goes to jail for these murders...."

"And you believe the *right* person is Scott," Sherri clarified.

"Maybe...maybe not," Lt. Jetro conceded, shrugging his shoulders. "Time...and the gatherin' of *all* evidence will tell us that."

"So along those same lines, you guys *are* lookin' for Jeanette, right?" Sherri pushed.

"Oh, yeah! You better believe it!" Lt. Jetro affirmed, rubbing his hands together as if anxious. "There are way too many open holes in our case without talkin' to Jeanette. You jest gave us another one with this note," he said, fingering the piece of paper on his desk again. "As you said, if Jeanette comes in for questionin', then we can do a comparison of the handwritin' on this note and his handwritin' on that day."

"Regardless of what your plans are for Jeanette, Lt. Jetro, we jest need to get him to come forward," Sherri pointed out. "I'd like for you to let me know when he comes forward and you question him. Can that be arranged?"

"I have no problem whatsoever with that, Sherri," Carter said. "Believe it or not, we are both workin' toward the same goal...gettin' a killer off the streets. And the sooner the better."

"That much you have my full agreement on," Sherri told him, sounding enthusiastic for the first time. "So how about we stop arguin' over *who* we think the most worthy suspect is, and concentrate on bringin' Jeanette Peterson in? I think, especially based on the way ya're leanin' the case, that I have a plan that might bring Jeanette out of hidin'. Interested in hearin' it?"

"Ya betcha," Carter said, laying down the pen he had been rolling in his hands and giving Sherri his full attention.

Since this Jeanette person seemed to be a master of disguise and a champion of flight, Carter realized he could use all the help he could get with flushing Jeanette out. Carter was more than happy to listen to Sherri's proposal. The sooner they could bring Jeanette in for questioning, the sooner they could either build a rock solid case against Scott or switch their emphasis to prosecuting Jeanette for the crimes. Whichever way, Lt. Jetro's primary goal was to get a brutal killer off the streets once and for all. His ears anxiously awaited Sherri's plan.

Chapter 13

The Heat is On

The next day, Carter received a call from District Attorney General, Rance Dooley. This call was far from the first Carter had received from this man. Ever since Jameson Thornton had been murdered, Rance had been breathing down Carter's neck to bring him a feasible suspect. Rance wanted this case solved, and he wanted it solved *yesterday*. Gatlinburg was a town known for tourism and not homicides, and Rance wanted to keep it that way.

"So how's your murder investigation coming for the Jameson Thornton homicide?" Rance wasted no time asking.

Silver-haired, blue-eyed Rance was sitting behind his large desk looking out the window at the snow that was blanketing Sevierville. Five more inches were supposed to fall in the area before it was all done. The Smoky Mountains always looked so beautiful covered in snow.

Even though Carter had found it humorous that Rance had referred to the homicide by name – it was the only homicide he was working – Carter's voice was all seriousness as he shared, "My circumstantial case against Scott Arnold is growing stronger," Carter shared.

Rance was aware that Carter had been leaning toward charging Scott Arnold with this murder. "How strong of a case have you got?" he probed. "Is it time for me to convene a grand jury and you to issue an arrest warrant?"

"Not quite yet," Carter admitted with hesitation.

"Why not yet?" Rance pushed, his impatience coming through loud and clear.

"I still have some holes I need to fill," Carter told him, tapping a pen against a pad of paper on his desk.

"Well, maybe I can help you fill those holes, or maybe we can just find a way to step around them," Rance suggested, rocking back in his chair and tapping his fingers together. "The mayor wants this case solved, Carter, and so do I. He doesn't like for folks in Gatlinburg to feel afraid. Right now, it's much more than the snow that's keeping some people away, and we can't have that. We need to show everyone again that they have absolutely nothing to fear in this area. And naturally, the way to do this is to bring a killer to justice. I think it's time we met and you show me just what you've got on Scott Arnold. It's time for me to start building a case against our killer. Don't you agree, Lieutenant?"

"Definitely," Carter concurred, moving his head up and down. "When do you want to meet?"

"This afternoon...two o'clock?" he suggested.

"Sounds good," Carter readily agreed

"See you then," Rance said.

They ended their call. Carter was not averse to meeting with Rance. He found the D.A. to be a very open-minded, fair individual. Carter believed that Rance would do everything in his power to help bring this case to justice, and Carter believed he needed Rance's help to accomplish this important feat. Carter was looking forward to his two o'clock meeting with the D.A.

Chapter 14

The Broadcast

A week later, on December ninth, at ten-forty-five p.m., Wallace Cleaver was sitting on the couch in his den watching the end of some detective show when a news preview caught, and riveted, his attention. He grabbed the remote and turned the volume up a notch.

Knoxville's, Channel 2's, dark-haired, immaculate, middle-aged anchor, Clifton Reed's, teeth sparkled as he announced to the camera with relish, "A suspected serial killer is *now* behind bars! Tune in to News Channel 2, at eleven, for all the details on the arrest of Scott Arnold for the murders of Jameson Thornton in Gatlinburg, Joe Butler in Pigeon Forge, and a string of other murders, not only in Tennessee but Kentucky as well." A short clip of Scott in handcuffs, being led away by a Sevier County sheriff, was played before the news clip ended and a commercial for toilet paper was broadcast.

Wally perched on the edge of his sofa, caressing the end of the remote with his thumbs. *Can it really be so?* he wondered. His body happily quivered as he accepted, *It has to be. I just saw and heard it with my own eyes and ears.*

As the detective show came back on, Wally wished he could fast forward through the rest of it. He could not wait to see the news and what further details they would provide on the arrest of Scott Arnold. Wally was so thrilled by this information that he could not sit still. He waited in agony, fidgeting, and looking at the clock every two minutes until the closing credits for the detective show finally rolled.

Wally rocked back and forth and exhaled several times as he waited through another series of commercials. Then, at last, Clifton Reed's smiling face appeared onscreen again. Wally's mouth salivated. He rubbed his hands together and peaked his ears as Clifton's voice rang out saying, "And in our leadoff story tonight...."

As Clifton rattled in the background, saying essentially the same words he had in the news preview, the news station quickly ran the film of Scott being arrested that Wally had already seen. It was only when Channel 2 cut to the clip of Rance Dooley, Sevier County District Attorney General, that Wally sat up and took notice again.

A long, grey, winter, men's dress coat with matching grey, leather gloves covered Silver-haired Rance's body and protected him from the cold. The only other items of clothing showing were the collar of his light blue dress shirt and the knot from his navy silk tie. Rance stood in front of the Sevier County Courthouse. Several media microphones were in front of him. His dark blue eyes shared a love affair with the cameras as he told the public at large, "After significant evidence was presented by Gatlinburg detective Lt. Carter Jetro and Pigeon Forge detective Lt. Pete McCoy, an indictment was handed down against Mr. Scott Arnold of Hendersonville, Tennessee for the murders of actor Jameson Thornton and Joe Butler. It also appears that Mr. Arnold was likely involved in murders occurring in Nashville and Hendersonville, Tennessee, as well as in Louisville, Kentucky. Mr. Arnold has been taken into custody and awaits arraignment tomorrow morning. A trial date is expected to be set as soon as possible."

As the camera switched back to the studio and Clifton Reed, the reporter added, "Channel 2 has been asked by local police and the district attorney's office to broadcast a plea in connection with the arrest, and prosecution, of Scott Arnold. Police are looking for a woman last known by the name of Debbie Gray. When last seen, she had medium-length black hair and green eyes. Debbie is about five-foot-seven and weighs about 175 pounds. It is believed that Debbie Gray may have useful information crucial to the prosecution of Scott Arnold for these crimes. Police ask that, if Debbie Gray is in the area, she please come forth for questioning. Again…they stress this woman's testimony may be crucial to Scott Arnold's prosecution. If anyone knows of the whereabouts of this woman, please contact Lt. Carter Jetro in Gatlinburg or Lt. Pete McCoy in Pigeon Forge. Let's all work together to make certain this dangerous killer is off the streets for good," Clifton added, looking very concerned and earnest.

As Clifton's female co-anchor, a large-breasted blonde, rushed on to the next news story, Wally settled back on the couch and let what Clifton had said sink in. *Police are looking for Jeanette, but only to question about* Scott's *murders?* He considered with strong misgiving. *Can I trust this?* He wondered.

Wally knew exactly where they could find Jeanette, a.k.a. Debbie Gray. He marveled at the fact that police seemed to be building a strong case against Scott for *all* the murders that had occurred. Wally had only set Scott up for the latest two murders. Since he had not been able to kill Scott that night on the railroad bridge, he had schemed to get rid of him in a different manner; through having him prosecuted for murder.

Is Jeanette really off the hook for all the other murders? He questioned. *I need to make absolutely certain before I make any moves toward the police talking to him.*

Wally realized, only too well, that if he made the wrong move, things could come toppling down right on top of *him*, and he could not take the chance of this happening. *I'll hang back and see what else transpires with Mr. Arnold. Then, if I feel confident the police really have a solid case against him, I might throw Jeanette into the mix. Especially if it helps to get Scott prosecuted for* all *the murders. Life is good!* he concluded with delight, leaning back on the couch and allowing a riotous laugh to erupt.

Chapter 15

The Visit

A few days later, Sherri walked through the front doors of the Sevier County Jail building with a heavy heart. After going through a metal detector, she was led by a corrections officer to a private prisoner visiting area. The walls of the small room – about the size of a walk-in closet – were painted a drab gray, and it was lit by the minimum of fluorescent lighting. Sherri felt an odd sense of claustrophobia as she took a seat in a black plastic chair and stared at an *empty* chair and a *closed* door on the other side of a glass partition.

A moment later, Sherri watched as the door opened and Scott shuffled into his half of the blocked off room. He was dressed in the typical black and white, striped, cotton, short-sleeved shirt and pants issued to Sevier County Jail inmates. Scott had dark circles under his eyes. His chin and upper lip were covered by a two-day growth of dark black hair, and the hair on his head was tossed and tangled, looking badly in need of a comb.

Scott's haphazard appearance twisted Sherri's heart. As she reached to pick up a telephone receiver from the unit hanging on the wall beside her, Scott took a seat in the chair facing Sherri. He extracted his headset as well.

"Hi. How ya doin'?" Sherri asked with a bittersweet smile. She placed her other hand on the glass.

Scott raised a hand and placed it on the glass in the same spot as Sherri's. They both sadly realized that this action was as close as they were going to come to touching. "I'm doing alright," Scott tried to assure Sherri, but there was no sign of a smile on his face, and his eyes looked much too unhappy.

After a few seconds, they both removed their hands from the glass and settled back in their chairs.

"I hate that ya have to be here, Scott," Sherri whined, her eyes remorseful.

"Believe me…I hate being here too, Sherri," Scott confessed, glancing down at the short ledge in front of him. Looking back up at Sherri, he forced a silly smile and tried to lighten things up a bit, rotating his head back and forth and saying, "But a man's gotta do what a man's gotta do, right? So tell me…any leads on Jeanette's whereabouts yet?"

"Lt. Jetro and the D.A., Rance Dooley, are pullin' out all the stops to try and track down Jeanette. They have actually contacted the FBI to see if a national plea can be aired for him to come forward. Although, I believe, as you do, that Jeanette is hidin' in plain site, somewhere in this area."

"I could almost guarantee it," Scott agreed, absently shaking his head up and down. "Hopefully, it won't be too much longer before Jeanette comes forward, even though they are treating me okay here. Since inmates don't like ex-cops too much, I've been provided with my own private cell. And even though the grub is questionable…I haven't found too many bugs in it yet…."

"Gross, Scott! Cut that out now!" Sherri demanded, waving her hand, looking down, and shaking her head. Looking him back in the eye, she assured him, "We are all workin' together to see that Jeanette comes forward as quick as possible. I'm goin' ta see to it that your innocence is proven, Scott. I miss you!"

"I miss you too, Mrs. Arnold," Scott said, reaching to touch his fingertips to the glass again. It frustrated him greatly that he could not even touch his wife.

Sherri kissed her fingertips and touched them to the glass where Scott's rested. She fought tears. It was killing her seeing Scott in jail, and since Christmas was less than two weeks away, she knew they would likely spend Christmas parted. Their separation made Sherri all the more resolved to see that Jeanette was brought in for questioning. Sherri truly believed that Jeanette's reemergence was the first step to proving Scott's innocence. And this very thing could not come fast enough for her.

* * * *

When Wally sat down to dinner that night, his attention was, all at once, diverted away from the curly-haired, four-year-old girl sitting across from him to the television on the kitchen counter. He grabbed the remote and turned up the volume as he watched a video of Sergeant Sherri Ball-Arnold walking out the doors of the Sevier County Jail building.

As the camera switched back to the news channel studio, anchor Clifton Reed eyeballed the camera and flawlessly read his cue cards, reporting, "Sherri Arnold, Scott Arnold's wife and a detective with the Hendersonville Police Department, was spotted by Channel 2 News leaving the Sevier County Jail after visiting her husband today. Local police and the D.A.'s office are still seeking a woman last known by the name of Debbie Gray."

Then the cameras cut away to a clip of district attorney Rance Dooley standing in front of the Sevier County Courthouse again in his winter coat and gloves. Standing tall and looking confident, he told a host of reporters, "As all of you already know, suspected serial killer Scott Arnold is currently being held in the Sevier County Jail. At his arraignment, he was denied bail because of the viciousness of the crimes he is being charged with. Taking into account the upcoming holidays, a trial date has expeditiously been set for January second of next year. The D.A.'s office is seeking the collaboration of a woman last known as Debbie Gray. It is believed that Ms. Gray could play a pivotal role in the prosecution of Mr. Arnold. I'd like to make a personal plea, once more, for Ms. Gray to come forward as soon as possible. The Sevier County D.A.'s office has a wealth of evidence proving Mr. Arnold's guilt, but Ms. Gray could serve as the nail in his coffin. Help us put away this dangerous individual once and for all."

As the cameras came back to the studio, and Clifton's blond bimbo co-anchor rambled on with another unrelated story, Wally smiled, turned down the volume on the television, and focused his attention back on the four-year-old sitting at the table with him.

"Eat your peas, Susanna," he directed, knowing the little girl was finicky about eating green vegetables.

Wally picked up a knife and sawed into his rare steak. He licked his lips as he watched the red juices run across his plate. *I think it might be time to get Jeanette involved in all this*, he concluded. Wally knew he would like nothing better than serving as the 'nail in the coffin' for Scott Arnold.

Chapter 16

The Informant

The next day, an older model, black, diesel pickup truck, with flames painted down the sides and a bush bar in front, rumbled into the parking lot of the Pigeon Forge Police Department. Pulling the truck into a parking space a few rows back from the door, a large man, with long grey hair that was pulled back in a braided ponytail, threw the truck into park, ground out a cigarette in the ashtray, and shut off the ignition.

Climbing out of the vehicle, he stowed his keys in the empty front pocket of his worn jeans. A chain hung from his other front pocket. The other end of the chain was attached to his wallet that was inside a back pocket.

He sunk his nicotine stained hands into the pockets of his weathered, black, leather jacket, slammed his truck door, and made long, determined strides toward the front door of the police department.

Once inside, he approached the information counter and asked to speak with Lt. Pete McCoy. He told the woman behind the counter that it was in reference to the Joe Butler homicide.

A few moments later, Lt. McCoy joined this stranger in the entrance foyer. "Hi, I'm Lt. Pete McCoy," the lieutenant introduced himself, offering his hand.

"My name is Kurt Preston," the other man told him, shaking the detective's hand. Kurt scrutinized the slender man whose hand he had just shaken. He noted that Lt. McCoy wore his jet black hair a bit long and that his tie was loosely knotted. These observations relaxed Kurt a bit. He did not really like being in a police station. Even though Kurt had never been arrested, he had still had some nasty run-ins with the law when he had been younger.

"So...ya wanted to speak with me regardin' the Joe Butler homicide?" Pete wasted no time asking.

"Yes, sir," Kurt said with respect. "Is there someplace private we cain talk?" he asked, glancing around him. There was no one else in the lobby at this time, but Kurt knew this scenario could change at any time, and he did not really wish for his conversation with the lieutenant to be overheard.

"Shore," Pete agreed, sweeping his head up and down. "Lit's go to my office."

"Sounds good," Kurt agreed.

The two vacated the lobby. They took a nearby elevator to the second floor. Going through a door that had a sign reading *Homicide Division* on it, they passed a re- ceptionist, who barely gave them any notice. Lt. McCoy stopped at the next door on the right and directed Kurt to go inside this room. Stepping inside, Kurt headed toward the lieutenant's desk. Pulling back one of two chairs that sat in front of the desk, Kurt had a seat. Pete shut the door, went around, and settled into the chair, behind his desk.

Kurt observed the certificates on the wall behind Lt. McCoy's head. He also took note of pictures on the lieutenant's desk. One he assumed was a picture of Lt. McCoy and his wife, and the other two pictures, one of a small boy and one of an older girl, he guessed to be the lieutenant's children.

"So what cain I hep ya with today?" Pete asked Kurt.

Kurt shifted his focus from the items in the office to the lieutenant's interested face. "I have informat'n that I feel might be related to the murder of Joe Butler," Kurt revealed, shimmying in his seat.

"What kinda information?" Pete asked, folding his hands in front of him.

Kurt looked down and ran his finger over a yellowed fingernail on one of his hands. Looking back up at Lt. McCoy, he cleared his throat and said, "I ain't no saint. Not by any stretch of the imagina'n. But I cain't jest sit by and possibly lit an innocent man go to prison."

"Are ya talkin' about Scott Arnold?" Pete guessed, looking Kurt directly in the eye. It was obvious that something gravely bothered Kurt about Scott Arnold's possible conviction.

"Yeah," Kurt agreed, nodding. "I don't know what ya've got on that guy, but I think ya need to know that there was another pretty strange individual lurking around on the day Joe Butler was murdered. In fact, I seen this other man goin' in Joe Butler's room dressed as a security guard. And comin' back out a littl' later dressed in regular street clothes with a trash bag in his hand."

"Did ya recognize this other man?" Pete asked, sitting up tall in his chair. His grey eyes were full of curiousity.

"Uh...yeah," Kurt slowly revealed, glancing down into his lap again. Meeting the lieutenant's eyes, he added, "This same oddball came into my office earlier that day to find out the name of the man and woman who often rent room 105 on Friday. He gave me fifty bucks for their names. He came back a little later that day and rented room 105 for an hour. Then after his hour was up, he came back to the office and said he wanted to rent room 205, across the way, for three hours. I thought all this was a littl' odd, since I never saw nobody else with him. Usually it's couples that rent our rooms by the hour," he further explained.

"What did this man look like? Can you give me a descript'n?" Pete asked. He slid open his drawer and pulled forth a notepad. He also reached to extract a pen from a coffee cup full of pens sitting in the middle of his desk.

"Normally, I might not have noticed what the guy looked like. But this guy was a bit odd lookin'," Kurt shared. "His facial features reminded me more of a woman than a man. He was kinda short and a littl' on the heavy side. He had bleached blond hair that was spiked with gel, and his eyes were a strange...greenish brown color. I think he had in some of those contacts that change the color of yer eyes. Know what I mean?"

"Only too well," Pete agreed. "What was the name this man checked into the hotel under? Do you remember?"

"Oh, yeah!" Kurt replied, leaning back in his chair and crossing his arms. "It would be a littl' hard for me to forgit the name he give me. The man signed in under the name of Scott Arnold. Now, isn't that jest the oddest coincidence for an alias?" Kurt stated with a doubtful smirk on his face.

"Yeah, I'd say it was," Pete agreed, pinching his bottom lip between his index finger and thumb.

"If the Scott Arnold ya have in jail rally murdered Joe Butler, I'd say this other man was in cohoots with him, and needs to be punished too. But jest between you and me, I think the Scott Arnold ya have in jail is an innocent bystander who jest happened ta find Joe Butler's body. I think this other dude, who stayed in both room 105 and 205 the same day as Joe, butchered Joe and set Scott Arnold up to take the fall. That's why I'm comin' forward. I'm not gonna jest sit by and lit this other weirdo get away with cold-blooded murder. Not on my watch!" Kurt told him, a hard frown on his face.

"I appreciate ya comin' forward with this informat'n, Mr. Preston," Pete told him. "I'm guessin' ya wouldn't mind testifyin' in court to what you observed?"

"If it means gittin' a killer off the street, then I'm down with testifyin'," Kurt agreed, shaking his head up and down.

"Good. I need to git yer contact information then," Pete told him. "Do ya have an ID on ya?"

"Yep," Kurt said. He raised up from his seat and extracted his wallet. Pulling forth his driver's license, he handed it across the desk to Lt. McCoy.

Pete took a second to record Kurt's information on his notepad. Then he handed Kurt back his wallet. "And a telephone number I cain reach ya at?" Pete asked.

"909-0001," Kurt rattled off.

Pete jotted the number down under Kurt's contact information. Then looking him back in the eye, he said, "I need to call the D.A. with this new information."

"Sounds like the man that should know all this," Kurt agreed. He slid back his chair and stood. "I'll git outta yer hair. I've said all I've come to say. I hope it heps."

"I definitely think it will," Pete told him, flashing him a grateful smile. "Can ya find yer way out?"

"I'm sure I can," Kurt told him, reaching to grab the doorknob. He opened the door and stepped into the hall.

"Thanks again, Kurt," Pete called after him.

"Sure thang," Kurt said and disappeared down the hall.

Pete wasted no time picking up his phone, but before he called the D.A. to relay his information, he called Gatlinburg police detective Lt. Carter Jetro.

Chapter 17

Presumption of Guilt

Three days later, on Monday, December fifteenth, at two in the afternoon, Lt. Jetro received a call from the information booth in the lobby of the police station. The man at the desk told him, "Lieutenant, there is someone here who says they need to speak with you regarding the Jameson Thornton and Joe Butler murders."

"I'll be right out," Carter told him. He was curious to see who wanted to talk to him and what they had to say. Information in homicide cases was always welcomed, even if some of it did turn out to be bogus.

Opening a door, Carter stuck his head into the lobby. The man in the information booth pointed to the stranger in the lobby and Carter watched as a five-foot-seven, stocky man with short, spiked, blond hair and greenish brown eyes turned toward him. The man was dressed casually in jeans and a pullover sweater. He had a winter jacket draped over his arm, having just come from outside.

Carter could not help but notice that the man looked eerily like the description Lt. McCoy had given him of the strange individual that had camped out at the Adam Ridge Motel the day Joe was murdered. Keeping this fact in mind, Carter eagerly motioned with his hand for the man to approach. After the man had walked through the door, Carter allowed it to close. Then he offered his hand saying, "Hi. I'm

Lt. Carter Jetro. I understand ya wanted to speak with me regardin' the Thornton and Butler homicides."

"Yes, sir," the blond-haired man replied, nodding, the slightest hint of a smile curving the corners of his lips.

Carter did not find it odd that this man did not introduce himself. He knew he would eventually find out the identity of this man, but he would not push it. The last thing he wanted to do was spook this individual before he found out what he had to say regarding the murders. "Well...how 'bout we go to my office and talk," Carter offered and started down the hallway.

"Sounds good," the stranger agreed, following closely at Lt. Jetro's heels.

They passed several other desks; some vacant, but most occupied. A few of the individuals at the desks gave Lt. Jetro and the stranger a curious, passing glance as they walked by, but most of these people were focused on other things at their desks. A woman in ratty jeans and a concert T-shirt walked up the hall toward them. Lt. Jetro paused a moment and asked her, "Any luck?"

"You betcha," she replied with a proud smile, skipping off down the hall.

"One of our undercover officers," Lt. Jetro briefly explained to his visitor, as he came to a stop beside an opened door. A black name tag, with white lettering, hung in the center, high on the door. It read: Lieutenant Carter Jetro, Homicide. Carter held out a welcoming hand, ushering the stranger into the room. Before Carter entered, he asked the man, "Would ya like somethin' to drink? We have some soft drinks in the frig or there's a water cooler..."

"No thanks," the man replied. He rolled back an office chair, draped his jacket over the back, and had a seat in front of Lt. Jetro's desk. This stranger studied the few stacks of paper on the lieutenant's desk and noted how neat they were. He noted a picture of the lieutenant in uniform with other officers, but he saw no sign of pictures of a wife, girlfriend, or children. He wondered if the lieutenant was an old bachelor, or if he was just not sentimental about family.

Carter walked into his office and pulled the door closed behind him. He darted off to the side of his visitor, going behind his desk, and settling into his matching cloth office chair. He sat at an angle where his computer monitor did not block his view of the man sitting across from him. Sunlight coming through the window behind Carter reflected what looked like contact lens in this stranger's eyes. Since the man's eyes were a unique shade, Carter believed his visitor's contact lens were tented.

Leaning back in his chair to give the impression that he was relaxed, Carter wasted no time asking, "So what cain I do for ya this afternoon, Mr…um…I'm sorry…I don't believe I got your name." Carter folded his hands in front of him and patiently waited, gauging whether his question seemed to make his visitor uncomfortable or not.

"No, you didn't," the stranger said. Looking like the cat that had just swallowed the canary, a wide smile canvassed his face. "Not that you would know it from looking at me…but I'm the person you guys have been looking for," he revealed tapping his thumbs against his chest.

Carter's eyes narrowed and his forehead furrowed. "I'm not sure I follow what ya are gettin' at, pal. Can ya clear up the confusion for me a littl' bit?" he asked, separating his hands and holding them out to his sides, palm up.

"You betcha!" his visitor said with enthusiasm, rubbing his hands together in front of his chin. "Lt. Jetro, allow me to officially introduce myself," he said. Bending forward, he stuck his hand across the desk, grandstanding, "I'm Debbie Gray."

"Uh…Ya're…" Lt. Jetro stuttered, his eyes squinting as he barely touched the man's hand. He gave the man across from him a hard stare. Looking closely, he could ascertain certain effeminate traits about this man now. His chin and lip line were too smooth, looking not clean-shaven but as if it had always been hair free. The curve of his lips was more like a woman's. His body held no muscle where a man's should. And his voice was a bit high-pitched for a man's.

"I'm Debbie Gray," the stranger repeated, sitting back in his chair and folding his hands over his abdomen. There was a smug expression on his face.

"O…kay," Carter replied, sitting back in his chair himself, folding his hands in front of him again, and swiveling from side to side. "So I take it ya have had a sex change. Because…quite frankly…the woman that was described to me as both Debbie Gray – and Jeanette Peterson – was voluptuous. And you look completely flat-chested to me."

"I did have a sex change," Debbie admitted, chuckling and tapping one hand on top of the other. But he quickly clarified, "It was actually years ago when I was a teenager though. This time around, the surgery just…sort of…well…set things right. I don't suppose you've ever heard of a disorder called Reifenstein Syndrome?" he asked, rolling his thumbs.

"Cain't say as I have," the detective answered, bringing a hand up to his chin and hooking his bottom lip with a finger. His dark eyes stared holes through the *man* in front of him as he fully concentrated on what he had to say. Carter was eager for this individual to continue.

"Reifenstein Syndrome is a disorder that causes the body to reject all male hormones. So even though I was born a boy, I always looked like a girl...even down there," Debbie said, pointing between his legs.

Carter tried not to flinch as Debbie's words sunk in. "So ya were one of those children that were both a boy and a girl," he concluded, moving his hand to rub the side of his face by his temple.

"Yep," Debbie agreed, exhaling and grimacing. "That was me. And it gets even better! You see, when I started to mature, my parents decided that even though I had undeveloped testicles that had not fully descended, I was *still* a girl. They would not accept the fact that I might actually be a boy. They even went so far as to have the testes removed and a breast augmentation done. So from that point on, I was a man trapped in a woman's body. As I said, this latest operation just...somewhat...set things right. Now, I at least look like a man, even though I still cannot function as one."

"O...kay," Carter dismissed, clearing his throat and tapping a knuckle to a lip. This man's last words gave him more information than he really needed to know. "So ya look like a man now...physically...yet you still introduced yerself as Debbie Gray. Surely ya are not still goin' by a woman's name."

"You're very perceptive, Lieutenant," Debbie praised with a half smile. "But then again, I guess you have to be in your line of work. No, I don't still go by Debbie Gray. I only introduced myself to you as such because I knew you were looking for me in this manner."

"So what's your given name these days?" Carter continued to dig, picking up a pen and pushing a pad in front of himself.

"You know, with that pen and paper in front of you, you remind me of a psychiatrist I used to see in Nashville. Especially since you appear to be a lot older than I expected you to be," Wally commented, taking a hard look at the lieutenant's thinning hairline and pudgy belly. "My psychiatrist was a bit chunkier and had a lot less hair...."

"Dr. Wallace Cleaver," Carter filled in the blanks with a knowing grin, clicking his ballpoint pen.

"Very good, Lieutenant. You've done your homework. Wally was a great guy...."

"Indeed," Carter interrupted, pointing the pen toward Debbie. "He tried to kill for you from what I've heard and ended up losing his life in the process."

"Yeah, it was ironic that Wally became violent, when he counseled me on how to control my anger in a non-violent manner. He died much too soon. That's one of the reasons I decided he deserved to be resurrected," Debbie admitted, tapping her thumbs.

"Resurrected?" Carter questioned, raising an eyebrow.

"Yeah. You see, I go by the name Wallace Cleaver now. That's what I legally changed my name to after the surgery," he said, tapping his chest with the palm of his hand. "I look at this as a fitting tribute to a great man. Even if Wally did go a little nuts in the end, his heart was in the right place. Wally only wanted to help me. He knew Scott was threatening me, so he decided to try and eliminate the threat. He wanted me to be able to go on with my life without being harassed."

Carter reached up to rub one side of his forehead. All of the radical twists and turns in Debbie's, a.k.a. Wallace's, dialogue were beginning to give him a headache. "Lit's backtrack a little, Wallace," he suggested, purposely switching names. "Ya mentioned that Dr. Cleaver was counselin' ya on how to control your anger in a non-violent manner. What happened when yer anger came out in a violent way?"

Wally grinned and touched the knuckles of his folded hands to his chin before replying. "Well...I can certainly tell you what did *not* happen. I didn't go around carving people up with knives, like Mr. Arnold would have you believe."

"Now how do ya know that Mr. Arnold is goin' around bad mouthin' ya like that, Wallace?" Carter questioned, scratching behind an earlobe.

"I came to that conclusion while I was still living in Louisville. That's why I left and changed my identity. Scott showed up in Hendersonville. He's damned and determined to ruin my life. I'm just glad Scott Arnold is finally behind bars where he belongs," Wally stated, pointing both his index fingers at Carter and shaking them.

"And why exactly did ya feel so threatened by Scott's wild accusations? After all, what proof could he possibly have against ya to back up his bizarre claims?" Carter asked, laying down his pen and sandwiching his hands in front of him.

"Scott Arnold was a police detective when he started harassing me in Louisville," Wally stated. Then he apologized, "No offense to you, Lieutenant. I'm sure you are an honorable law enforcement official, but Scott Arnold was not." Squeezing the arms of his chair, Wally added, "Who knows what kind of evidence he might have conjured up against me."

"I can tell you that he found yer DNA at two of the crime scenes," the detective confessed, purposely not defining in what form the DNA was found. Carter carefully studied Wallace's response to this information. He noticed Wallace rolled his eyes up, which meant he was carefully formulating his response.

Looking the lieutenant directly in his daunting eyes again and tapping his fingers on the arms of his chair, Wally finally asked, "Which two crimes scenes?"

"Chad Kennison and Mitchell Peterson," Carter revealed.

A smile once again formed at the corners of Wally's mouth. *What perfect two victims*, he mused. "The fact that my DNA was found on these two men does not come as a surprise to me, Lieutenant. You do realize that Mitchell Peterson was my husband, right? I heard you mention my real name, Jeanette Peterson, earlier in our conversation. So I figure you uncovered that fact in the extensive research you done on this case. And that same research had to have revealed that Mitchell was my husband."

"It did," Carter confirmed, bobbing his head. "But yer DNA was found in the hotel bed where he was murdered. And not only Scott Arnold, but his partner, Roger Matthews, reported that they talked to you after Mitchell's murder and that you thought he was out of town. They reported that you were shocked that he was found at a hotel in town. So how is it that yer DNA was discovered in the bed in that room? Can ya explain this?" Carter interrogated, glad to be getting to the meat and potatoes of their discourse finally.

"I *was* shocked that Mitchell was in that hotel room," Wally confirmed. Then looking down, exhaling and rubbing his head, he looked the detective back in the eye and said, "This is a bit embarrassing, but I guess nothing is sacred when it comes to Scott Arnold's distortions of the truth. I *was* in that hotel room with Mitchell...."

"Whoa! Wait a sec!" Carter protested, putting his hands up palm out. "If ya was in the room with him, then why didn't ya tell Detectives Arnold and Matthews this when they brought you news of your husband's death. Roger Matthews said that yer grief seemed authentic."

"It *was* authentic. I cared a great deal about Mitchell. The two of us were trying to have a normal life together. Another facet of Reifenstein Syndrome is that you have virtually no sex drive... So, I can swing both ways in my attractions. And I can also love both sexes. I loved Mitchell, even if I wasn't sexually attracted to him. The sex thing did present a problem in our marriage though. So I did things to spice up our sex life. Mitchell and I got together with swingers on an ongoing basis, and sometimes we would role play. We were role playing the day he died…"

"So did he ask ya to strangle him during sex? Was that a way of spicin' things up?" Carter asked, picking up his pen again and unconsciously shaking it at Jeanette.

"Yeah…it was," Wally confessed, his cheeks coloring. He looked down in his lap and rubbed one thumb over the other.

"So what happened? Did it get out of hand, and ya ended up stranglin' him to death?" Carter probed, squeezing his pen between his hands.

Wally's head jerked up, his eyes narrowed, and he shook his finger, as he angrily contested, "No, it did *not*! He was alive and well and sound asleep when I left him. He still had his tie around his neck, but it was loose. He was breathing just fine. Whoever killed him did so *after* I left. And they made it look like all the other murders by adding the handcuffs and the knife."

"And ya think this *someone* was Scott," Carter suggested, holding his pen lengthwise between his hands and leaning his chin on it.

"You guys are the ones that arrested Scott for murder, and it's been reported that he is also a suspect in the other murders in the Nashville area and in Kentucky. So *you* guys must believe that Scott is the one who killed Mitchell, as well as the other victims. So what's it matter what I think?" Wally asked, sounding a little defensive.

"Well, if we didn't care what ya thought…or might know…then why would we have broadcast an appeal to have ya come forward?" Carter argued, his eyes dark pinpoints of light.

"If that's the case...then yes...I believe Scott Arnold murdered not only my husband but *all* the victims. I think he's a real psycho and should be put away for life...or maybe even put to death," Wally shared, tapping the arms of his chair again.

"Okay...there's only one other thing I need for ya to clear up for me..." Carter said, scratching the back of his ear.

"What's that?" Wally asked, looking suspicious. He had his hands in loose fists now.

"No need to get uptight," Carter told him, reading his body language.

"I'm not uptight. I'll be glad to clear up any loose ends so I can...what is it the reporters were saying on television? ...put the final nail in Scott's coffin. Sounds good by me," Wally said, hostility spewing from his mouth.

"Okay. Then I need to ask ya...what about the DNA that was found at the Chad Kennison murder site? Can ya account for this?" Carter inquired, caressing his pen between his hands.

"Yeah," Wally said. Then he looked down in his lap again. Looking up and meeting the lieutenant's intense gaze, he began to explain, "I met Chad Kennison while he was serving on jury duty. I was the assistant jury administrator. He was a real playboy. He kept asking me out. I told him I was married, but that did not seem to faze his advances. Finally, I agreed to go with him one evening to a nightclub in downtown Louisville called Petrus. From the time we got there, Chad was all over me. When I finally got tired of fighting his roving hands and mouth, I coaxed him into the alley. I'll be honest with you, knowing he would be into the kinky stuff, I handcuffed him to a pole in the alley, and then I...well...I gave him a blowjob. I left him handcuffed in the alley with a big 'ol smile on his face. I figured there were enough people around that someone would come by and get him free. I never guessed he would be murdered."

"Once again, why didn't you share this informat'n with detectives Arnold and Matthews?" Carter asked, looking suspicious for the first time.

"I was a married woman who was out on a date with a young stud. Not exactly something I wanted getting back to my husband…"

"But I thought ya said you loved Mitchell and were trying to build a life with him. Why go out with another, younger man then?" Carter dug a little deeper.

"It was a moment of weakness. As I said, my lack of sex drive was an issue between Mitchell and me. Mitchell was turning a cold shoulder to me because I was turning down his sexual advances, and here was this young stud in hot pursuit of me. I just went to Petrus with him to prove to myself that I was still desirable."

"Why were ya carryin' around handcuffs?" Carter probed, sliding his pen back and forth between his hands.

"Well, not because I'm a mass murderer that carries them around and uses them on my victims," Wally contradicted, fanning his hands out to the side. "Actually…they weren't my handcuffs…they were Chad's. He tried to handcuff me to a lamp in the nightclub, and he wanted me to go to a nearby hotel with him and let me handcuff him there while we had sex. Like I said, this young man was into kinky stuff too."

"Sounds like," Carter agreed, shaking his head up and down in agreement. "It takes all kinds in this world," he commented, seeming to accept Wally's story lock, stock and barrel. "I'm glad we talked and you cleared up these items,

Wallace. I only have one more quest'n for you. Would ya be willin' to testify for the prosecut'n at the upcomin' trial of Scott Arnold?"

"You know it!" Wally was quick to agree, a wide smile covering his face.

"Okay. I need to get some contact informat'n from ya so the DA's office can contact ya," Carter said, picking up his notepad and clicking his pen and laying it on top.

Carter rose up a little from his chair and held the notepad and pen out to Wallace. Wallace rose from his chair and took these items. "Don't you want to see my ID?" he asked, curiously studying the lieutenant.

"Of course," Carter confirmed, bobbing his head. "But if you would, write down your contact information first. I'll confirm it all with your ID after you are through," he told him, sitting back down in his chair and settling in.

Without hesitation, Wally wrote down his name, address and phone number on the small notepad Carter had handed him. When he was finished, he rose out of his chair, extracted his wallet, and pulled forth his ID. Handing the notepad, pen and ID across the desk, Wally watched as Carter stood and gathered the items.

Carter placed Wally's ID to the side of the notepad and seemed to be carefully crosschecking the information on it with the information on the notepad. A moment later, he handed Wallace back his ID and had a seat again. With a trace of a smile, Carter asked one final question. "Mind if I ask what you do for a livin'?"

"No. Not at all," Wallace replied as he rose up, pulled out his wallet, slipped his ID back inside, tucked his wallet into his pant's pocket again, and sat back down. "I'm a security guard at Dollywood."

"Back to workin' security, huh?" Carter commented with a half smile. "Ever see Dolly Parton at the park?"

"You betcha!" Carter replied with a proud smile. "I've been a personal security guard for her and other stars as well. That's one of the perks of working there."

"Sounds like," Carter agreed, nodding his head. Rising, he added, "I so appreciate ya comin' forward today, Wallace. I believe ya can help us get Scott Arnold off the street once and for all."

"I certainly hope so," Wally said as he slid back his chair and stood, pulling his coat from the back of the chair and draping it over an arm.

Carter walked over to his office door. Opening it, he said to Wallace, "I'm sure the D.A.'s office will be in touch."

"I look forward to the call," Wally told him with another wide grin as he meandered past Carter, out the door into the hallway.

"Thanks again for coming in, Wallace," Carter said, reaching to shake Wallace's hand.

"It was my pleasure," Wally said, enthusiastically shaking Carter's hand. "I'd do just about anything to get Scott Arnold off the streets."

I wonder if that includes murder, Carter found himself pondering. "I'll walk you out," Carter offered, vacating his office and shutting the door.

The two men set off down the hallway toward the exit door. Carter was anxious to get Wallace Cleaver out of the building. His brain was still actively processing all the irregularities in the statement Wallace had just given him versus the ones he had given Scott Arnold and his partner.

Even more damning, Carter could not help but notice that the loops and strokes in Wallace's written account of his name and address bore a haunting resemblance to the loops and strokes in the note Sherri had given him. Coincidentally, Carter had been looking again at the note Sherri had given him just before Wallace had arrived.

After his lengthy talk with Wallace Cleaver, the handwritting sample he had gathered, and Wallace being a dead ringer for the man that had been identified coming out of Joe Butler's room the day he was killed, Carter had serious doubts about Wallace Cleaver a.k.a. Jeanette Peterson's innocence and even more grave doubts about Scott Arnold's guilt.

Chapter 18

The Trial

As scheduled, Scott's murder trial began on January second. As Wally sat down to his dinner with Susanna that night, he learned his first details about the trial from his favorite news anchor, Clifton Reed.

As a picture of Scott in his black and white jail scrubs was flashed on the screen over Clifton's right shoulder, the reporter sat behind his anchor desk with his hands folded in front of him, every shiny, black hair on his head in place, and flawlessly read from his cue cards, "The homicide trial of suspected serial killer Scott Arnold began today with a surprising twist."

The news station cut to a clip of district attorney Rance Dooley then. In a pressed, gray, pinstriped suit, light blue dress shirt, and navy silk tie with gray diamonds, Rance stood in the hallway, outside the closed doors to the courtroom where Scott was being tried. As usual, there were several microphones in front of his face.

Rance announced to the community, "Because Scott Arnold's trial is such a high profile homicide case, with movie star Jameson Thornton's death being scrutinized, I petitioned Judge Rudy Ledgewood today for a closed trial. Judge Ledgewood agreed. So not only will there be no live media coverage within the courtroom, but no spectators will be allowed in the courtroom during proceedings. Only those giving testimony that day, jury members, lawyers and court officials will be allowed in the courtroom each day. But don't fret," he said to the press with a half smile. "I'll be sure to keep you guys posted on the outcomes of the trial each day. The D.A.'s office is confident we will have a conviction against Mr. Arnold in a prompt and speedy manner."

Giving equal time to Scott's defense attorney, next, Channel 2 turned their cameras onto Roland Miles. Tall – six-foot-five, and lanky, depending on one's perception, Roland either looked like an ex-basketball star or an ostrich. Not only was Roland peculiar looking, but he was also an odd duck to be defending Scott in such a grievous homicide trial. Roland was a defense attorney, but he was only twenty eight years old. Since he had not been an attorney long, he had tried mostly civil cases and not criminal, and even with his civil trials, Roland had only a so-so track record for wins. Scott's choice of attorney had the press, and the public at large, scratching their heads and speculating on Scott's lack of wisdom in choosing Roland as his attorney versus a recognized criminal attorney with an established record of wins.

The press' attention centered on Roland now; he came across as unprepared and insecure in giving interviews as well. He had his suit jacket unbuttoned, his hands thrust deep in both his pant's pockets, and he was bouncing up and down on his toes. His interview could have given a viewer motion sickness if it had lasted very long. Fortunately, the news clip was only a little over a minute long.

"Um…I'm confident that…uh… Judge Ledgewood's decision to have a closed trial was…well…was a good one. I'm certain my client will soon be found innocent of all charges," Roland proclaimed to the cameras, giving no hint of how he intended to prove Scott's lack of guilt.

The cameras switched back to the news station then and Clifton Reed's gleaming white teeth. "Channel 2 will have more details of this important trial, day by day, as it unfolds," he promised his adoring public.

As usual, the cameras panned to his delectable, busty, blond co-anchor next and her coverage of the next important news item of the day, and at that same moment, Wally turned the volume down on his television and focused his time and energy on sharing dinner with Susanna. Wally did not know whether to be happy or not about the judge's decision to have a closed court for Scott's trial. Regardless of this decision, though, Wally was happy about Scott's choice of bumbling attorney. Wally could envision Scott's prosecution for the murders more and more each day, and this fact greatly excited and pleased him. Wally was surprised that he had not been called upon to testify at Scott's trial, but he supposed the detective he had talked to would relay his information in court. Wally could hardly wait for Scott's trial to commence.

* * * *

Wally religiously tuned into the news each night to see what was being reported on Scott's trial. Each night, there was a report from D.A. Rance Dooley and also a report from Scott's attorney, Roland Miles. Each night, Rance Dooley's case seemed to grow more solid, while Roland Miles defense seemed to be falling apart. Roland always came across as unconfident and uncertain. Scott Arnold seemed doomed to a future in prison, and this fact made Wally almost delirious with happiness. He counted the days as Scott's trial grew closer and closer to it culmination.

* * * *

Two weeks after it had begun, Scott's trial was concluded. The jury was sequestered, and Scott, the attorneys, and the engrossed public, largely including Wallace Cleaver, anxiously awaited the verdict.

No one had to wait long. The jury was only out one day.

So that night, when Wally sat down to dinner and Clifton Reed's smiling mouth announced with glee, "A verdict has been reached in the Scott Arnold serial killer case", Wally could hardly breathe. He sat on the edge of his kitchen chair, with his fists clenched, fixated on the television set. His insides trembled as he fought not to shout, "Come on, give me the damn verdict!" Less than a moment passed before Clifton was speaking again, but it seemed like years to Wally because he was so overly eager to hear what the jury had decided.

Clifton's baritone voice relayed, "The jury unanimously found Scott Arnold guilty of the murders of movie star Jameson Thornton and local resident Joe Butler."

"Yes!!" Wally shouted, springing to his feet and dancing a little jig.

Clifton was still talking in the background, saying, "Mr. Arnold will also be tried in Davidson County for murders occurring in Hendersonville and Nashville, Tennessee, and in Louisville, Kentucky for murders occurring there. Judge Rudy Ledgewood is expected to hand down Mr. Arnold's sentence tomorrow."

Wally was not really listening to Clifton now. He had heard the information that he needed to hear. Scott Arnold was going away to prison, and this fact thrilled Wally to the core.

Looking over and seeing Susanna's eyes studying him with bewilderment, Wally shuffled over to the little girl and grasped both her hands. "Come on, Susanna. Dance with, daddy!" he prodded. Susanna slid out of her chair and allowed her daddy to spin her around and around a few times. She was giggling and a little dizzy when he finally released her. Wally dropped to his knees and pulled his little angel into his arms. "It's all over, Susanna," he told her.

"What, daddy?" she mumbled, confused.

"The bad man who tried to have you taken away from me is going to prison, Sus. He can't hurt you or me anymore. We're free, baby! We're free!" he gushed, shaking her back and forth some more.

Susanna did not fully understand what had happened, but glad to see her daddy so happy, she was happy too. She smiled and laughed and rejoiced with her daddy.

Chapter 19

The Lure

On January twentieth, three days after a life sentence was handed down to Scott by Judge Ruby Ledgewood, a black Buick LaSabre pulled into Wallace Cleaver's driveway in Wear Valley, Tennessee at six p.m. Wear Valley was about eleven miles from Pigeon Forge and just twenty miles shy of Gatlinburg. So, as Sherri and Scott had assumed, Jeanette had been hiding in plain sight all along.

Sherri cut the ignition, turned off her headlights, and opened the driver door of her LaSabre. Climbing out of the warm vehicle into the cold – nineteen degrees with a wild chill hanging near zero – Sherri shivered, even though she donned a long, wool, winter coat. But even though it was bitterly cold, Sherri realized her body tremors were not only from the artic air but from nervous anticipation of meeting with Jeanette, a.k.a. Wallace Cleaver.

Slamming her car door, Sherri walked, in the dark, up the side of the driveway, approaching the sidewalk leading to the front porch. She had ascended a single concrete step and was making her way up the walk when her path was suddenly illuminated by a porch light. Sherri's attentive ears also picked up the sound of a deadbolt being turned; she guessed Wallace was unlocking, and not locking, the door. Sherri took a deep breath and prepared for her face-to-face encounter with this dangerous man.

As Sherri stepped up the first half step leading onto the porch, the front door and the screen door swung open, and standing in the lighted doorway was a small-framed man in sweatpants and a sweatshirt. This man had spiked golden blond hair and greenish brown eyes. There was a gloating smile on his face.

"Sherri! So good to see you again," he proclaimed with a chuckle. Stepping back a step and holding the screen door open, he invited, "Come on in, out of the cold, and visit for awhile, won't you?"

Sherri hesitated for only a moment. Then she climbed the other two porch steps and slipped past her crazy host and into his house. She stopped and turned in the entranceway, her eyes silently poring over Wallace Cleaver. It was still hard for Sherri to accept that Jeanette had surgically altered herself into a man now.

Wally shut the door and turned to face Sherri. When he did, he noticed her intense scrutiny. "Like my new look?" he asked, fanning his hands, palm out, at his sides as if to say, "Tada!"

"No. Not much," Sherri dared to reply, a hard frown on her face.

"Now, Sherri, don't come into my house and hurt my feelings," Wally warned, shaking his finger at her. But he was still wearing a half grin.

"Why? What will ya do to me if I do?" Sherri challenged. She placed her gloved hands on her hips and stared him down.

"What would you think I might do to you, Sherri?" Wally answered the challenge, his gaze serious for the first time.

"I think we both know the answer to that question, *Jeanette*," she said, purposely adding his female, given name to fan flames. It worked, because Wally's lips became a taunt line.

But Wally was wise enough to realize that Sherri was trying to incite his anger, hoping things would get out of hand with him, and he would say, or do, something stupid. That being the case, Wally cleverly changed the subject, saying, "You know…I'm being rude." Holding his hands out, he offered, "Let me take your coat."

Sherri slipped her purse off her shoulder and sat it on the floor at her feet. She removed her gloves, slipping them into the pockets of her coat. She watched Wally very carefully as she unbuttoned her coat and slid out of it. She handed the coat to Wally and picked up her purse and slung it over her shoulder. Sherri watched as Wally swiveled sideways, opened a closet in the hall, extracted a plastic hanger, hung up her coat, closed the door, and turned to face her once more.

"Why don't we get out of this entrance hall? I want you to feel comfortable in my home, Sherri. Susanna is in the den watching cartoons. Why don't we head that way? I'm sure you'd like to see how much she's grown since you tried to have her taken away from me in Hendersonville. She's had a little trouble adjusting to the fact that I'm her father now …instead of…well…being her mother. But Susanna adapts very well to change. She's had to, since Scott's had us on the run so much. But I guess all that's in the past now. Justice has finally been done with Scott going to prison for *all* those horrible murders. Susanna and I won't have to worry about being harassed anymore."

"I came here to talk about Scott…and the murders. Do ya really want to talk about these things in front of yer…" Sherri stopped herself short of saying 'daughter'. She just could not bring herself to refer to innocent little Susanna this way. She wished that Jeanette had not been able to get Susanna back. Sherri had managed to have Susanna put into protective custody for a short while when Jeanette had been suspected of the murders in Hendersonville.

"In front of my daughter?" Wally finished Sherri's sentence. "No. I don't want to talk about all *that* in front of her. That might give her nightmares, and as I said, Susanna's been through enough...moving from place to place...and adjusting to my new looks/genders. I only want you to peek your head in and see how precious she is."

Sherri realized Wally was only taking her to see Susanna to rub it in her face that he still had custody of her, and always would, and there was nothing she could do about it. Sherri played along with Wally's sick little game, even though she knew it would wrench her heart to lay eyes on this adorable little girl again and realize she was still living in the house of a monster.

At the end of the hallway, Wally stuck his head into the spare bedroom that acted as their den. "Sus, we have a visitor," he said.

A little girl, with a full head of flowing curls, sat on a carpeted floor a few feet from a television set. She turned her head, directing her attention from the cartoon she had been attentively watching to her daddy's smiling face.

"Say hello to Sherri, Susanna," Wally directed, stepping further into the room so that Susanna could get a good look at Sherri.

When Susanna's beautiful, golden brown eyes got a good look at Sherri, they grew large and troubled. Susanna sprang to her feet and dashed over to her daddy. She wrapped her arms tightly around one of his legs and buried her head into his thigh. "No! Don't let her take me!" she pleaded, obviously frightened.

"I don't think Susanna likes you very much, Sherri," Wally commented, a crooked smirk on his face.

"Enough with your cruel games!" Sherri warned in a low growl. "Why don't you let the child be and we can go to another room and talk in private?"

Sherri wanted to get out of Susanna's sight as soon as possible. She realized Susanna remembered that she had come to her house in Hendersonville and had taken her away to social services. The last thing Sherri wanted to do was frighten this poor little girl. Sherri was angry that Wally was torturing Susanna in this manner. His actions clearly showed that he was not fit to be this precious child's parent.

"It's okay, Sus," Sherri heard Wally soothe Susanna. He stroked the back of the girl's head. "No one is ever going to take you away again. Sherri just came here to tell us that the bad man that caused you to be taken away last time is the one whose been taken away. He's gone away to prison, so he can never hurt you, or anyone else, again."

Susanna pulled her head back from Wally's thigh and looked up at his face. "Are you sure, Daddy?" she questioned, giving Sherri only a frightened, fleeting glance.

"Positive, precious," he said. He bent down and kissed Susanna on her small, soft forehead. "You go on back to watching cartoons now. Sherri is going to go in the kitchen with me and we're going to celebrate the bad man going away and the two of us never having to run or be scared of anything again. Isn't that wonderful?"

"Yeah," Susanna agreed, her face brightening. Since her daddy seemed happy, all was fine with Susanna's world again too.

Sherri watched as Susanna pulled away from Wally, turned, and sat back down on the floor to watch her cartoons again. Susanna had completely dismissed Sherri's presence and the threat she had posed only minutes before. Susanna seemed to trust Wally a great deal. The girl seemed to accept every word he said to her as gospel. Sherri's heart twisted. Whether Wally was a monster or not, to Susanna he was her trusted, loved parent. *What a sad situation*, she could not help but conclude.

Wally slipped out of the room and motioned for Sherri to follow him back up the hall. When he came to the entrance to the kitchen, he reached inside to flip a switch on the wall and turn on the overhead dome light. Then he made his way over to the small, four-chair, kitchen table. Sliding out a chair, he had a seat, fanned out a hand, and invited, "Sit. Make yourself comfortable. You came for some reason, and I'm dying to hear what that is."

"I'll just bet ya are," Sherri said with a hostile edge to her voice. She walked over to the chair at a right angle to Wally, and lowered her purse into the seat. She clutched the top of the chair with both hands and stood staring down at Wally.

"Don't want to sit? That's fine," Wally said, shrugging his shoulders and holding one of his hands up backwards in the air. "So what's on your mind, Sherri?"

"I think ya have a pretty darn good idea what's on my mind," Sherri told him, no sign of a smile on her face.

"Hmm…let me guess," Wally said, briefly touching his index finger to his lips. Removing it, he continued, "If I had to guess… I'd say…Scott going away to prison, maybe? Am I warm?"

"Actually…for the cold fish ya are…ya're steamin' up the waters," Sherri told him, her lips pressed tightly together.

"What a poetic way of putting things, Sherri," Wally praised, lightly clapping his hands. "But how about we get on with our conversation while the night's still young? I don't want to rush you off, but I'd like to spend some quality time with my daughter before I have to put her to bed. So why don't you just say what you came to say. No more beating around the bush, okay?"

"Suits me," Sherri agreed, running a finger along the back of the chair. Locking eyes with Wally, she shared, "I actually came here to congratulate ya on your victory, *Jeanette*. Scott's been put away for the murders that ya committed, and he'll likely be in prison for many years…if he ever gets out. And with Scott locked away, that leaves ya free to kill again. After all, ya've gotten away with it once; why couldn't ya git away with it again?"

Staring back at Sherri, Wally replied, "I realize Scott is your husband, Sherri, so you're bound to believe whatever lies he has spread, but I can assure you that all Susanna and I want…all we have ever wanted…is to live a peaceful life. And life will be much more peaceful with Scott Arnold behind bars and out of our lives for good."

"That I don't doubt," Sherri agreed with a forced smile. "In fact, yer life should be copasetic without Scott lurkin' around keepin' a close eye on yer every move. There's only one hitch in the giddy up that I know of," Sherri revealed, a small twinkle in her eye.

"Okay, I'll bite," Wally said with a slight smile. "What might that *hitch* be?"

"That *hitch* is *me*," Sherri proclaimed, tapping a hand to her chest. "Scott may be goin' to prison, but I'm not goin' nowhere. I'll be there every time you turn around, watchin' your every move. I'll be Scott's eyes and ears while he's in prison, and sooner or later you'll slip up…that thirst for blood will be too great…and you'll kill again. And I'll be there to catch you, like a hook to a fish. You mark my words, *Jeanette*. I will get you!"

"Nice speech, Sherri," Wally praised, softly clapping his hands for a second time that evening. "You're a law enforcement officer, Sherri, so I'm sure you are aware that there are anti-stalker laws in this state. So if you harass me too much, I may have to call the authorities on you. I'd hate to see you wind up in jail too. That would be too sad."

"Trust me, ya'll never catch me followin' ya around or catch me harrassin' you. But ya still need to know that I'll always be in the shadows watchin' ya, *Jeanette*. I just want this understood," Sherri threatened, her face set like stone.

"Guess I better toe the line then," Wally said, smiling again.

"That…or be prepared to kill me," Sherri challenged, pulling back on the chair and raising its front legs off the ground a bit. "If I was killed while Scott was locked up…well…that would really be the cat's meow, wouldn't it? An ultimate revenge on Scott," Sherri suggested, sitting the chair level again.

"Wouldn't it though," Wally agreed, a flutter of excitement surging through him at the mere notion. He would love to make Scott Arnold suffer through the death of another loved one. Wally averted his eyes, fearful Sherri would see the passion in them for her suggestion.

"I figured ya'd like that suggest'n, Wally," Sherri commented, releasing the chair. "But just know I'll be closely watchin' my back too," she told him, swinging her finger at him. "I'd love for ya to try and close in on me for the kill, because as a police officer, I have a right to defend myself, and ya'd give me the opportunity I need to shoot ya dead. So I welcome the hunted…that's you by the way…to hunt the hunter…*me*," she said, tapping her chest. "Ya think about that, *Jeanette*. I don't plan on comin' to visit ya anymore, but I hope we meet up face to face again real soon."

"You're goading me, aren't you Sherri?" Wally asked with a wide, amused smirk.

"Ya bet yer sweet ass I am," she admitted. "I'll have my day with you, Jeanette…one way or the other."

"Does that mean your visit is over," Wally asked, pushing back his chair from the table.

"I think so," Sherri agreed. "I think I've said all I came to say."

"Indeed," Wally agreed, standing. "Let me walk you to the door and get your coat for you."

"What a plan," Sherri agreed, snatching up her purse from the chair seat.

Wally led the way out of the kitchen and Sherri followed. In the entranceway, Wally opened the closet and retrieved Sherri's coat. Closing the door and taking a step toward Sherri, with a chuckle and a toothy smile, he dared to say, "Hope to see you again *soon*, Sherri." Then he placed her coat in her hands and stepped aside, so Sherri could make her way to his front door.

"Ditto," Sherri said, staring him down with her steely eyes as she juggled her purse and pulled her winter coat on. Buttoning it, she started for the front door.

Once she had stepped out onto his porch, Wally said, "Drive safe, Sherri. Thousands of people are killed each year in traffic accidents. I'd hate for you to become one of those casualties."

"Bet you would," she commented. "I don't plan on going anywhere anytime soon, *Jeanette*," she pledged.

Giving him one last steely glare, Sherri took long strides down the sidewalk and along the side of the driveway. Extracting her remote from her purse, she pressed a button and her driver's side door clicked unlocked. Pulling the door open, Sherri hopped inside her vehicle, locked the doors, and started the car. A moment later, she shifted into reverse and backed out onto the street. As Sherri placed the car in drive and started away, she took one last glance at her nemesis, Jeanette.

He still stood in the lighted doorway watching her drive away with an eerie, wicked smile on his face. Wally even dared to raise a hand to wave goodbye to Sherri. She stepped down on the accelerator and raced away, hoping, and praying, her challenge to Jeanette had been strong enough to cause his killing juices to boil again. So many futures depended on this scenario unfolding as planned.

Chapter 20

Curiosity Killed the Cat

Wally's telephone rang the following evening at seven p.m. Wally was sitting in the den watching television while Susanna lay on her belly, working away with several crayons on a picture in her coloring book. Wally reached over and fumbled for his cordless phone that sat on a small table to the side of his recliner. Thinking the call might be from some telemarketer, Wally's attention was still largely centered on the television. Pushing the talk button, he murmured, "Hello."

"Hi, Wallace," a vaguely familiar voice replied. Then the caller quickly identified himself, saying, "This is Lt. Carter Jetro from the Gatlinburg Police Department."

"Lt. Jetro," Wally acknowledged, sitting up tall in his chair. Wally reached for the television remote and hit the mute button, silencing the television. His full attention was on this call now. He wondered with a tinge of trepidation why the lieutenant was calling *him*. After all, Scott had been sent to prison for all the murders in the local area, and trial dates were supposed to be being set for Scott to stand trial for the other murders as well. *So what's Lt. Jetro want with me now?* Wally had to wonder.

"So how's it been goin', Wallace?" the lieutenant asked, sounding more like a friend than a law enforcement officer.

"It's been going great, Lieutenant," Wally replied, sounding upbeat. "Any day that Scott Arnold is in prison is a good day."

"It is indeed," Carter agreed, his voice chipper. "That's the reason I called, Wallace," he admitted.

"To talk about Scott's imprisonment?" Wally questioned, a hint of skepticism in his voice.

"In a roundabout way. I actually called to thank ya for helpin' to imprison this man," Carter clarified. "We appreciate ya comin' forward and sharin' what informat'n ya had. Your informat'n helped the D.A. build a rock solid case against Scott."

"Why wasn't I called to testify?" Carter asked. He had been curious about this fact for some time now. He hoped the lieutenant could shed some light on his question.

"I supplied the D.A. with all of the informat'n ya shared with me. I don't know why he chose not to call ya as a witness. But evidently, his strategy worked, because Scott Arnold has been convicted and is behind prison bars where he belongs."

"Amen to that!" Wally cheered, raising his voice a notch in celebration. Susanna looked up at him, so Wally gave her a calming smile and directed in a quiet voice, "Keep coloring, sweetheart."

Susanna obeyed without argument. More interested in coloring than her daddy's conversation, she lowered her head and concentrated on her coloring book once more.

"Does yer daughter need yer attention?" Carter asked, having heard Wallace speak to someone else.

"No. She's fine," Wally replied. Wally did not want his call with Lt. Jetro to end just yet, and he did not want to allow Susanna to be a distraction. So he slid out of his chair, stood, and walked out of the den and into the hall, softly closing the door behind him. Walking down the hall toward the kitchen, Wally asked, "So, Lieutenant, tell me, do you think Scott will be convicted of the murders in the Nashville area and in Kentucky as well?"

"I think that's a given," Carter answered with conviction. "But be advised…jest because ya weren't called to testify by our D.A. doesn't mean ya won't be called by one of the other D.A.'s. That won't be a problem for ya, will it?"

"Not in the least," Wally was quick to assure Carter. "Scott Arnold is guilty as sin of these other murders as well. He deserves life sentences for these crimes as well. And I'm more than willing to do everything in my power to see that he gets these sentences."

"Good. Glad to hear it, Wallace!" Carter said, sounding almost mirthful.

"Lieutenant, would you do me a favor?" Wally asked, flicking a switch and turning on the ceiling light in the kitchen. He walked over and pulled out a chair from the kitchen table and had a seat.

"What's that, Wallace?" Carter asked.

"Quit calling me Wallace. I prefer to be called Wally," he told him. Wally felt comfortable talking to the lieutenant now, and he wanted to relay this message to him by allowing him to call him by his shortened name.

"No problem, *Wally*," Carter said with a chuckle. "And ya can call me Carter, if ya like."

"I appreciate that, Carter," Wally replied, smiling. He felt like he had made a friend in law enforcement now. Scott's imprisonment had opened a lot of doors for Wally.

"I'm sorry Scott Arnold caused ya so much grief, Wally. I'm glad we were able to convict him and put him away where he cain't hert anyone else."

"Me too," Wally agreed. "Now, if you can just get his wife off my butt…"

"Sherri?" Carter interrupted, sounding surprised.

"Yeah," Wally confirmed. Then he commented, "I see that you are on a first name basis with her as well."

"Jest between ya and me, Wally, I'm workin' on bein' more with Sherri than jest on a first name basis. She's a looker, that one," he stated, sounding a little breathy.

"So when's the last time you talked to Sherri, Carter?" Wally asked, intrigued, and a bit disturbed, by Carter's last tidbit of information.

"Yisterday," Carter replied. "She dropped by the station about quarter to seven."

She went by the police station to see Carter after *she came to visit me*, Wally ascertained, intrigued. "Did Sherri tell you that she had come by my house first?" Wally asked Carter.

"No. But that don't surprise me much," Carter shared. "That darn woman's still got it in her head that Scott Arnold is innocent. I bet she is still tryin' to point the finger at you, ain't she? Ya know she tried to git me to work with her to have ya convicted for the murders in this area instead of Scott. But after ya came in and cleared up all the doubt about the DNA evidence they supposedly had against ya, the D.A. saw no reason to pursue ya at'll. All fingers pointed right as Scott then. Sherri is still not acceptin' that fact. But it's well past time she did, and I'm goin' to do everythang in my power to see that she forgits Scott Arnold and moves on with her life."

"Moves on with her life with…*you?*" Wally questioned, rubbing his index finger under his lip. He was finding this conversation most interesting.

"Lit's hope," Carter remarked. "The way I see it, Sherri is as good as a widow now. Scott will be locked up fer the rest of his life. And a lovely thang like Sherri deserves better than to be tied down by someone like Scott. She's done nothin' wrong…nothin' that is but git involved with a derelict like Scott Arnold. The way I look at it, Sherri is lucky to be alive, and she's needs to go on livin' and let Scott Arnold rot in prison whare he belongs."

"I quite agree, Carter," Wally concurred, his head absently bobbling. "I'd love to have Sherri off my tail. And if her chasing your tail accomplishes that, so much the better," he said with a snicker. "So do you think Sherri is attracted to you at all, Carter? Think she'll be into older men? Have any idea why she came by your office last evening?" He nosed around.

"Ya ask a good question, Wally," Carter told him. "I'm not rally shore why Sherri come by my office yesterday evenin'. She jest seemed to want company. And fer the first time, she wha'nt rally talkin' about Scott. And along those same lines, we're supposed to have dinner Friday night."

"You dog! You're moving right in, aren't you Carter?" Wally said, chuckling again and slapping his thigh. "So is Sherri driving back to Gatlinburg, or are you going her direction?"

"Sherri's comin' to Gatlinburg," Carter told him. "In fact, she's comin' to my house around seven o'clock. I'm cookin' for her. And hopefully…afterwards…she'll cook for me, if ya know what I mean," Carter insinuated with a hearty laugh.

"Don't move too fast, old buddy," Wally warned. "I get the feeling that Sherri is not a woman to be messed with…."

"I get the feelin' that Sherri is jest the woman I'd like to mess with," Carter told him, still being quite lewd. "I'm not goin' to rush anythang with her though, Wally. But sometimes a little seduct'n goes a long way…especially with a woman with a broken heart. And Scott Arnold has pretty much trampled lovely Sherri's heart."

"That's for sure," Wally agreed, bobbing his head again. "So where do you live, Carter? Are you right in Gatlinburg?"

"Funny ya should ask, Wally," Carter replied. "Ya see, I have myself a little, one bedroom, log home up off a Sky View Drive. Know where that's at?"

"Not exactly. But I haven't explored the area a lot since moving here. I pretty much go into work each day and then back to Wear Valley," Wally admitted.

"I hear ya," Carter agreed. "If I wasn't a police officer, I probably wouldn't know the streets as well as I do either. At least you have a littl' girl to keep you runnin'. I'm jest an old bachelor."

"Never been married?" Wally inquired.

"Nope. But shore have enjoyed playin' the field," Carter told him, laughing. "Anyway…my house is off from traffic light number ten in Pigeon Forge. Ya go one mile to the first bridge that turns to the left. Ya go one mile up King Branch Road. Then ya turn right onto Silver Poplar. Ya stay on Silver Poplar about two miles and then you turn right again onto Sky View Drive. Up a gravel drive that winds through a grove of trees, ya'll find my shack. 1905 Sky View Drive; that's me. Sounds complicated to git to, but now days, all anyone has to do is type my address into good ol' mapquest, and it'll, lickity split," Carter said, snapping his fingers. "route ya right to my front porch." Carter paused and took a breath. Then he added, "When the weather gits nicer, Wally, ya might have to come over some night. We'll kick back on my porch and enjoy a few brewskis."

"Now, I'll definitely have to take you up on that, Carter," Wally said. He had a pencil in his right hand and was looking down at a piece of scrap paper on the kitchen table. Wally had just jotted down quick directions to Carter's house as well as his house number. He could not believe Carter had run off at the mouth so much about the exact location of his home, but then again, Wally had found that folks in Gatlinburg and the surrounding areas tended to be very trusting…and very naïve as well.

"Geez, Wally," Carter said, exhaling. "I've jest been jabberin' on and on. I jest called to thank ya again for helpin' put Scott away. I didn't mean to keep ya on the phone so long."

"No problem, Carter," Wally said. "I've enjoyed talking to you. I'd love it if you would call me and let me know how your date with Sherri goes. As I said, your future with her will likely affect my future as well. Maybe if Sherri finds another love interest, she will leave me alone once and for all."

"Well…if I have anythang to say about it she will. I'll do everythang in my power to see that Sherri puts Scott Arnold, and anyone, and everythang, associated with him, behind her."

"Well, needless to say, I'll be rooting for your relationship to take hold then," Wally told him, rubbing his hands together.

"Startin' this Friday, Buddy," Carter said with confidence. "If I have anythang to do with it, Sherri Arnold will be spendin' the night in my bed, and this will be the beginning of the end of her obsession with Scott Arnold. You watch and see, Wally."

"I might just have to do that," he said, underlining Carter's address.

"Well…I'm gonna lit ya go. Ya go enjoy bein' with yer little girl now. Nice talkin' to ya, Wally."

"Nice talking to you, Carter," Wally said, smiling. "Goodbye."

"Bye now," Carter said.

Wally listened as the connection was broken. He stared down at the notes he had written. "I just may have to pay ol' Carter and Sherri a visit Friday night," he schemed aloud. Wally's curiosity about what might transpire between Carter and Sherri was far too great for him to ignore.

For now, Wally left his notes on the table, arose, turned out the light, and headed back down the hallway to the den to spend some time with Susanna before he put her to bed for the night. Wally knew he would be counting the days – two – until Friday evening rolled around.

Chapter 21

The Cover of Darkness

It was hours before Sherri and Carter's official *date* was to begin, but Sherri was already at Carter's house. Knowing Sherri was lonely and missing her man's touch, Carter opened up his home early to Sherri. Carter truly believed that Sherri deserved happiness in her life, so he was glad to be able to provide her a place of refuge for some much needed intimacy.

The roaring fire in the large cultured stone fireplace in the middle of Carter's great room was not the only thing giving off significant heat that afternoon. Two individuals, greatly in need of one another's touch, came together. Swept away by heightened passions, they kissed, embraced, fondled, and left a trail of discarded clothes as they stumbled off to the bedroom. Piling up in Carter's king-sized bed, they came together with renewed urgency, two individuals becoming one. Carter had accomplished his goal of bringing Sherri happiness, and the glorious smile spread all across her face was living proof of this fact.

* * * *

As if Sherri's blissful, contented smile were not enough, down lighting from two large, cast-iron, potholder chandeliers lit Sherri's face. She and Carter stood over a butcher block in the middle of Carter's kitchen, preparing dinner together. "You have a wonderful home here, Carter,"

Sherri gushed, looking up from the sharp gleaming knife she was chopping carrots and cucumbers with for their salads.

"Thanks. I like it a lot," he said, flashing a smile of his own. Then Carter went right back to focusing on the steaks he was doctoring with spices and juices for their main entrée. He had already placed a few potatoes in the oven to bake. The steaks would not take long to cook on the large George Forman Grill that sat on his countertop.

Carter's police radio/scanner beeped just as he was washing his hands in the kitchen sink, after having placed the steaks on the grill. Pressing a button, he spoke into an intercom, "Lt. Jetro here. What's ya got?" he asked, tingling with anticipation.

"Suspect's on the move," a male voice reported.

"Excellent! Can you tell yet if they're headed in the direction of my house?" Carter inquired, glancing at Sherri. He could tell she was eager to hear the news as well.

"Ten-Four. Suspect is in Pigeon Forge, headed toward traffic light ten."

"Well...yee ha!" Carter cheered, fisting his hands and shaking them. He noticed Sherri was grinning from ear to ear. "Report back when he gets close to the house. Okay?" he said.

"Ten-Four," the undercover officer responded once more.

"Sherri, if you would, watch the steaks, okay?" Carter requested. "I like mine pink inside," he added. Then as he started for the great room, he told her, "I'm goin' ta turn on some mood music. We'll eat in front of the fire, and then maybe we can share a dance or two. How's that sound?"

"Sounds marvelous!" Sherri cooed, practically floating over to the grill. Their plan was finally coming together. Sherri hoped upon hope that tonight would be the beginning of the end for Jeanette.

* * * *

Wally slowly drove his car along Sky View Drive. Fortunately there was not a lot of traffic on this road. There was a car behind him, but these folks seemed to be in no hurry, hanging well back from him.

Wally strained his eyes to read the numbers on mailboxes along the side of the road, even though he had his headlights set to bright. Sky View Drive, being a rural road, was very dark, with street lights only located sporadically along the route.

"1903!" Wally chirped out loud, even though he was alone in the car. Excitement surged through him as he recognized, *The next turn off should be Carter's shack.*

Wally slowed his car to a crawl. The car in back of him caught up, but still did not ride his bumper. Glimpsing a mailbox with *1905* on it, Wally's brain registered with zest, *There it is!* He also saw the turnoff for Carter's gravel driveway.

Wally steered his car over to the side of the road. The car behind him slowed almost to a stop; then they accelerated and headed around him and on down the road. Wally carefully pulled his car well off the shoulder of the road.

Shifting the car into park and extinguishing the headlights, Wally reached for the door handle and opened his driver's door. The ground was hard and frozen under his feet. Wearing a long black winter coat, hood and gloves, he was completely camouflaged by the darkness surrounding him. Making his way over to the turnoff for Carter's house, he crept up the side of the gravel driveway.

* * * *

The front of Carter's house was mostly windows, and these large windows had no shades or curtains. When Carter had decided to have his log home built, many years ago, he had also determined he wanted nothing – but logs, windows, and doors – between himself and the wonderful, outdoor sights and sounds of nature. Of course, all of these unobstructed windows also meant that, at night, when the lights were on in the house – as they were now – someone on the outside had an excellent view of what was transpiring inside the house.

Wally now stood several feet from the house, in a grove of trees, shielded somewhat from harsh January winds. He pressed a small pair of binoculars to his eyes, and he watched as Carter and Sherri sat on a bearskin rug in front of the fireplace with plates of food in their laps. They also drank what appeared to be red wine from long-stemmed glasses. Seeming very cozy with one another, Carter would occasionally stick his fork in a piece of steak on his plate and feed it to Sherri. Sherri would seductively slide the meat off of Carter's fork, licking her lips and smiling. Wally could vaguely hear the sound of soft music playing inside.

Carter's certainly going all out to set the tone for romance, Wally ascertained. Carter's seduction of Sherri came as no surprise to Wally, since Carter had shared his plans for Sherri with Wally on the phone two days ago. What was surprising to Wally was Sherri's reaction to Carter's obvious wooing. Contrary to what Wally would have guessed, Sherri seemed to be welcoming Carter's advances. This peculiar behavior troubled, and irked, Wally. He never would have guessed that Sherri would be so easily led astray. Wally had expected more loyalty to Scott from Sherri. He was greatly disappointed, and even a bit angered, by Sherri's odd, improper behavior.

I guess it's easy come; easy go for Ms. Sherri, Wally decided. His aggravation heated his body and helped to keep him warm. He continued to watch the new couple.

After Carter and Sherri finished eating, Carter took Sherri's plate and silverware, stacked it on top of his, and sat these items off to the side. He stood then, offering Sherri his hand. Sherri reached to take Carter's hand and allowed him to help her to his feet. Then the two of them moved to the center of the room. Carter slipped his arms around Sherri and the two began to sway back and forth, obviously dancing.

Wally watched as Carter and Sherri danced for several moments, occasionally gazing into one another's eyes. Then he saw Carter make his move. Carter brought his lips to Sherri's, and not only did Sherri *not* pull away from Carter's advance, but she began to enthusiastically return Carter's kisses. Wally pulled the binoculars away from his eyes, not believing what he had seen. *Is Sherri really that big of a slut? After all, Scott has not been in prison all that long, and she is still his wife. Can she really be moving on so soon?* he pondered, exasperated.

Wally slowly put the binoculars back up to his eyes. Not only were Carter and Sherri still kissing, but their hands had begun to move. Carter was now stroking and squeezing Sherri's buttocks, and Sherri was caressing the back of Carter's head and his neck.

Unbelievable! Wally decided with distaste, lowering his binoculars a second time as he noticed he was grinding his hands into them. *My whole life I would have killed to have had one ounce of the love that I thought Scott and Sherri shared, and here Sherri is throwing it all away in the blink of an eye on some old geezer almost twice her age. That bitch deserves to die! Sherri had the nerve to challenge me to try and kill her when she came to my house. Maybe I should rise to the challenge,* Wally found himself seriously contemplating for the first time, suddenly furious.

A moment later, the light in the great room unexpectedly went out.

Damn! Wally silently cursed, realizing his voyeurism had come to an end. With the lights extinguished, he could no longer see anything that was happening in the house. This fact frustrated and enraged him all the more.

A moment later, Wally was startled when the front porch light was suddenly turned on. He darted behind a large tree and peeped around the side. *Surely they couldn't have seen me*, he thought with a moment's trepidation. *There is no way*, he quickly decided, settled himself down. *They were way too caught up in the moment to notice someone lurking outside*

A moment later, Wally's assessment of the situation was proved valid. He watched as Carter and Sherri stepped into the doorway of his cabin. Carter had his coat on now. Sherri took the time to place her arms around his neck and give him another prolonged kiss. "Ya hurry back now; ya hear?" Wally heard her say.

"Fortunately I'm not that far from Pigeon Forge," Carter told her, giving Sherri another quick kiss. "I'll make like the wind and be back in no time. You make yerself comfortable now. I have a whirlpool tub in the bathroom off of my bedroom. Why don't ya go and relax in that? I'll join ya when I git back."

"That sounds like a splendid idea," Sherri blathered, giving Carter one, final, parting kiss. "I'll be waitin' for ya."

"Be back soon," Carter promised as he hurried off the porch and practically jogged to his nearby car, which was sitting in the driveway by the side of the house. Sherri closed Carter's front door and disappeared back inside the house.

I can't believe Carter is leaving Sherri all alone in his house, Wally pondered with delight, listening to the gravel crunching under Carter's car tires as he hastily backed his car up the lengthy driveway. Wally saw Carter's headlights sweep through the trees and heard his engine accelerate as he pulled out on the highway and started away. *Guess it's just you and me now, Sherri,* Wally ascertained, a smile spreading across his face. *Don't guess I'll need these anymore,* he concluded, folding up his binoculars and dropping them into a coat pocket. *Wonder how water jets full of Sherri's chopped up flesh and blood will look massaging her naked body,* Wally found himself musing. Waves of extreme titillation swept through him, causing tingles from head to toe. His heart racing, Wally began to quietly make his way toward the house.

* * * *

Wally crept down the side of Carter's driveway, staying well back in the trees. Since he had no idea which side of the house the bedroom was on, Wally did not want to take any chance that Sherri might look out a window and catch a glimpse of him. The last thing Wally wanted to do was spook Sherri and put her on alert. The element of surprise was crucial.

Wally made his way around the back of the house. A security light from the house behind Carter's shown through the grove of trees separating the two lots. It provided the back of Carter's house with a bit of illumination. Climbing three wooden stairs, Wally ascended onto a deck. There was a light showing through a small, frosted window on the back, left side of the house. Wally guessed this room was likely the bathroom off of Carter's bedroom.

Wally slinked up to a set of French doors leading off the deck and into the house. He reached out and took hold of a brass door handle. Giving it a soft tug, Wally was delighted when he discovered that the door was *not* locked. *I can't believe Carter is a cop and he isn't wise enough to keep his doors locked*, Wally pondered. But he also recalled how forward Carter had been about giving out directions to his house. *I guess good ol' mountain boys are just very trusting*, Wally decided. Whatever the reason, Wally was just very happy to discover that the door was not locked.

He slowly pushed the door open, listening for any sign of a squeak. The hinges were, thankfully, quiet. As Wally stepped inside the door, finding himself in the kitchen, he softly closed the door behind him.

Wally's eyes were already adjusted to the dark, from being outside prowling around in it, and Carter's neighbor's light shone through the kitchen window, so Wally could fairly well make out the outlines of items in the kitchen. The one that most caught his attention was the knife block in the middle of the butcher block in the center of the room. Wally's lips spread into a huge grin as he carefully made his way over to that particular object.

Fingering the handles of the knives, Wally closed his hand over the largest one and pulled upward, extracting the knife. *This one should do nicely*, he deduced, careful not to cut himself as he gingerly fingered the sharp point.

As Wally turned and cautiously tiptoed out of the kitchen, across the dark great room, and toward the room on the left of the house, he trembled. Wally was feverish with anticipation of what was to come. Sherri's death would bring him delight beyond reason. It would be Wally's final payback to Scott Arnold for all of the agony he had put him and Susanna through over the years. Thinking about the anguish Scott would suffer over Sherri's death, Wally could hardly wait to reach Carter's bedroom.

Oh, Sherri, your death is going to be the sweetest yet! he concluded, salivating as he placed his hand around the bedroom doorknob. His insides fluttered as he felt it turn.

Chapter 22

Element of Surprise

Sherri was sitting on Carter's king-sized, log framed bed in his large, black, terrycloth robe. She had her legs under a blue comforter and her back supported by a crisscrossed timber headboard. Candles flickered on each of the rustic, log wood, bedside tables and on Carter's matching dresser. They provided a fair amount of light in the room.

As Wally slowly began to pull the door open, Sherri was not certain whether the door was actually moving or if shadows, generated by the firelight, were playing tricks on her eyes. A moment later, as Wally pulled the door open wider and revealed himself standing in the door, Sherri felt even more befuddled. Dressed all in black from his head to toe, and with candlelight casting creepy shadows all around him, Wally looked like the grim reaper. Sherri gasped and jolted.

Hearing a sharp intake of breath and catching sight of movement, Wally stopped with a start, just inside the dim room. Glancing toward the bed, he finally spied Sherri.

"Well...well. Who have we got here?" Wally said, a half smile appearing on his face. He placed his arm behind his back, concealing the knife.

"What are you doin' here, *Jeanette*?" Sherri asked in a growl, her brain finally registering his real identity. Sherri's mouth straight lined and her eyes narrowed.

"Now I think that's more a question I should be asking you, Sherri," Wally said, frowning and pointing with his free hand. "What is Scott Arnold's *wife* doing in another man's bed? Frankly, I thought you would be much more loyal to Scott than this, Sherri. Especially after the way you threatened me, on Scott's behalf, at my house the other day. What gives?"

"Whatever I do…or don't do…with Scott…or anyone else…is none of yer business, Jeanette. Ya don't belong here," Sherri hissed, seeming angered by Jeanette's presence and his condescending attitude.

"No, Sherri. It's *you* that don't belong here," Wally told her, stubbornly maintaining his belief.

"The thought of the likes of you bein' my moral compass is downright laughable, Jeanette," Sherri told him, forcing a laugh. "Ya're nothin' but a cold-blooded slaughterer!" she freely accused, gritting her teeth and shaking her finger at him.

"And you, my dear, are nothing but a heartless whore," Wally informed her, taking a few steps closer to the bed. Squeezing the handle of the hidden knife, he added, "And, Sherri, I don't think whores deserve to live."

"Is that why ya kill people, Jeanette? Because ya're outraged by their behavior? What in the world did yer first victim, Renee, do to set ya off so bad? She was just a wife and mother," Sherri pointed out, hunching a shoulder. "Don't ya ever want to talk to someone about the murders ya got away with committin'?" she challenged.

"I did that somewhat with Dr. Cleaver, and he ended up copycatting off of me," Jeanette revealed, a crooked grin on his face.

"He…what?" Sherri questioned, her brow furrowed.

"Believe it or not, Sherri, Dr. Wallace Cleaver was the person who murdered all the victims in the Nashville area," Wally confessed. "Or one of his personalities did. Turns out my shrink was crazier than me. How's that for a strange twist of fate?"

"Ya're tellin' me that Dr. Wallace Cleaver suffered from multiple personality disorder?" Sherri questioned, her eyes very skeptical.

"Didn't you wonder why one minute he beat Scott almost to a pulp and pinned him to the railroad bridge to die and then the next he became a savior to you guys?" Wally asked, cocking his head to the side like a confused dog.

Sherri had to admit that she *had* always wondered about the sudden change in Dr. Cleaver's demeanor that night. *How could a man go to such opposite extremes so fast, unless they were mentally off? But can I believe what Jeanette just said about Dr. Cleaver being the serial killer in the Nashville area?*

"You're thinking it all over, aren't you, Sherri?" Wally inquired, stepping to the end of the bed. He placed one hand on the log footrest. The other hand, with the knife, he still held behind his back. Wally looked even more like the angel of death looming over Sherri now.

"Dr. Wallace Cleaver did present some odd behavior at the end of his life," Sherri agreed, shaking her head up and down. "But I'm certainly not goin' to believe that he is a killer based on yer word, Jeanette. Ya lie through yer teeth more than ya tell the truth. Ya never did tell me why ya killed Renee. And what about Debbie Gray? What did she ever do to ya? Renee and Debbie were both sweet and lovable ladies. It shows what a monster ya are that ya killed these two. Some of the other victims, like Chad, Mitchell and more recently Joe Butler, were pigs. Their deaths are a little more justifiable…if there is such a thang."

"Yeah, I think there is such a thing as a justifiable death," Wally told Sherri, nodding. "And just for the record…I never killed anyone who didn't deserve it, and that includes Renee and Debbie…"

"So you admit that you killed these people as well as Chad, Mitchell, Jameson Thornton and Joe Butler?" Sherri questioned, sitting up tall in bed now. Intense eyes stared holes through Jeanette, Sherri's attention riveted on him now. Sherri was so close to having Jeanette say just what she needed him to say that she could hardly stand it. Her mouth was dry as cotton as she eagerly awaited the next words that would roll out of Jeanette's mouth.

"You know what, Sherri. You deserve to know the truth," Wally told her with a smug smile. "Yes, I killed all of those people. And they all deserved to die. I could explain to you in minute detail why each of them deserved to die, but I just don't have the time right now. You see…I need to do what I came here tonight to do before your new boyfriend gets back from town," Wally told her, pulling the knife from behind his back and holding it in front of him in clear view. The flickering of the candles made the blade appear to flash.

"So now ya plan to kill me as well, huh?" Sherri probed, staring at the large knife Jeanette held in front of him, anxiously swaying.

"Yes, I do," Wally told her with relish, actually licking his lips. "I had planned to give you a cleansing death in the whirlpool tub. But you're not in the room you were supposed to be in. But you know, Sherri…it's just as well. When Scott's hears of your death, he'll also have to deal with the fact that you died naked in another man's bed. A double whammy for Scott; so much the better!" Wally blathered away, cackling out loud. He was thrilled the way things had ultimately turned out.

"And what do ya think? That I'm jest gonna lay here and let ya carve me up with that knife?" Sherri pressed, kicking the comforter off her legs. It was obvious she was ready to take flight and also to fight for her life.

"No, Sherri. I never took you for an easy mark," Wally told her, shaking his head. "That's why I brought this," he said. Reaching in his coat pocket, he whisked out a pistol. "If you resist me, I'll shoot you. It doesn't matter to me how you die. I don't have to kill you the same way as the others. Scott's already gone to jail for the other murders and likely will be prosecuted for all the others you mentioned. So maybe my next string of murders will start with the tops of the victims' heads being blown off. What'll you think?" he asked, holding the gun up high, cocking it, and aiming directly as Sherri's forehead.

Suddenly the bathroom door bolted open. Wally jumped at the unexpected interruption and turned to see what – or who – had caused the commotion. He was shocked to the core when he saw who stood in the door. It was Scott Arnold.

"Wha...How?" Wally stuttered, turning the gun toward Scott instead.

Wally was further disturbed when the antler dome light in the ceiling suddenly came on, enlightening the room all the more, and an imposing voice boomed from the open doorway behind him, saying, "Drop your weapons, Wally. It's all over."

Glancing over his shoulder, Wally saw that Lt. Jetro stood in the doorway to the bedroom. He had his service revolver trained on Wally's back. "There's an officer outside that window acrossed from ya that won't hesitate to shoot his rifle right through that thar glass. So ya're completely surrounded. The best thang you can do now is drop yer weapons."

"You're supposed to be in prison," Wally said, still focusing his main attention on Scott. He shook his gun at him, and there was a totally bewildered expression on Wally's face.

"Well...allow me to clear things up for you, Jeanette," Scott said, a smile on his face as he took another step closer to him. "My arrest, arraignment, trial...all of that...it was all a sham. A sham devised by my beautiful wife Sherri," he said, fanning a hand out in Sherri's direction. "Lt. Jetro," he said, pointing over Wally's shoulder. "The D.A. and even the press. You see, Sherri and I knew you well enough to know that your gigantic ego would force you out of hiding if you thought you could stick it to me. Oh...and by the way, Jeanette. Sherri is wearing a wire. We've got your complete confession on tape," Scott told him.

Wally glanced over at Sherri. She had pulled her robe off to reveal that she was dressed in shorts and a strapless halter. Attached to the side of her shorts was a transmitter. The tiny microphone had been clipped to the lapel of her robe.

"Now *who* is going to rot in prison? Or if we are even luckier, roast in the electric chair?" Scott asked with a toothy, gloating grin.

"I guess that would be me," Wally answered. "But you know what else that means, Scott?" he asked.

"What?" Scott asked, wondering what garbage Jeanette would come off with next.

"I have absolutely nothing to lose," he remarked. There was a loud bang as Wally squeezed the trigger on his gun without blinking an eye.

As Sherri screamed, two more gunshots rang out and the window cracked. Sherri watched as Scott, clutching his left side, below his ribs, slowly crumpled to the floor. Blood was streaming from between Scott's fingers. As Sherri leapt from the bed and rushed to Scott's side, she did not even notice that Jeanette had been shot twice and laid, facedown, bleeding from both a head and back wound, at the foot of Carter's bed.

Sherri's only mission was to rush to Scott's side and tend to him.

"It'll be alright, Scott," she told him, bunching up her robe and tightly holding it to his wound. She also kissed Scott's forehead.

Scott slowly moved his head up and down, and tried to smile, but he quickly slipped into unconsciousness. Sherri did not like the amount of blood her robe was absorbing. She feared Jeanette's bullet might have hit a vital organ.

She looked over to see Carter on his mobile radio. "We need an ambulance ASAP," he barked. "We have two victims down. I repeat two victims down."

Carter walked over to Wally then, knelt down, took the weapons from his hands and tossed them far to the side. Then he felt for a pulse. Even though Wally was unconscious, his pulse was still strong. He hoped the same was true for Scott.

Why didn't I anticipate that Wally would shoot Scott? I should have taken Wally out before he got off a shot? he second-guessed himself, already feeling guilty.

Carter got to his feet again and went to help Sherri tend to Scott. He left Jeanette to the care of the other officers who had flooded into the room. Carter did not care if Wally/Jeanette lived or died. But Scott had to be alright. They had all worked together too hard, and planned too well, to have it all blow up in their faces now.

Come on, Scott! Hang on, man! Carter silently implored, helping Sherri to apply pressure to Scott's wound and hold off the bleeding until vital help arrived.

Chapter 23

Stay with Me

Two ambulances arrived about fifteen minutes later. The paramedics did a quick check of both victims' vitals, and then they posthaste loaded both Scott and Wally into their respective vehicles. Both individuals were immediately hooked up to oxygen, IVs, and monitoring devices as the ambulances sped away, sirens flashing and wailing, headed for Fort Sanders Sevier Medical Center, the only emergency care center in Sevier County. Sherri rode with Scott in the back of his ambulance, a death grip on his hand as she pleaded with him to stay with her. Carter had jumped in the back of the ambulance with Wally, wanting to be kept apprised of his condition at all times.

Sherri knew Scott had lost a lot of blood while they were waiting for the ambulances to arrive. She still had stains on her hands from where Scott's blood had seeped through the heavy robe she had been pressing with all her might to his wound. Scott's color was ashen and his blood pressure low. But at least Scott's heartbeat was still steady, and Sherri prayed it would stay that way.

"Come on, Scott. Ya've got to hang in there, sweetheart. They're goin' to fix ya right up at the hospital," she told him, fighting tears. "We've done what we set out to do. We've gotten Jeanette off the streets once and for all. Ya have to stay around and see her get convicted," Sherri rattled on, believing Scott could hear her even though he was out cold. "I love ya,

Scott. Ya cain't leave me. Ya hear?" she said, stroking his clammy forehead.

Hurry! Sherri's panicked thoughts screamed, wanting the ambulance to grow wings and fly. It took them less than fifteen minutes to get to the hospital, but this time seemed an eternity to Sherri.

When they finally arrived at the hospital, the paramedics, and Sherri, bolted into the gleaming, white, sterile, antiseptic-smelling emergency room with Scott's gurney. Wally's gurney was rushed in right behind. Carter stepped off to the side and watched as teams of medical professionals converged upon both victims like vultures after fresh prey. He found himself gravitating closer to Scott's gurney. Carter did not care so much what the doctors did for Wally, but he cared greatly that Scott got the best of care. Carter did not know how he was going to live with himself if Scott died. Carter intently watched Scott's medical team: a red-haired, youthful-looking man in a white coat and several others in scrubs.

"What have we got here?" Carter heard the redheaded man ask. He also noted the man's name – Dr. Malloy. The doctor's name was embroidered in red on the left-hand side of his coat.

One of the paramedics rattled off Scott's case to the physician, "Unconscious, twenty-nine-year-old male with a gunshot wound to the abdomen. Blood loss substantial. B.P. has remained stable at eighty over fifty. Heartbeat is shallow."

"Okay. Curtain one to prep for immediate surgery," he instructed, pointing.

Carter watched as the individuals in scrubs swiftly pushed Scott's gurney away in the direction the doctor had indicated. He caught sight of the forlorn expression on Sherri's face as she looked on in the direction Scott had been taken. He took a few steps closer to Sherri and the doctor.

"Are you that gentleman's wife?" he heard the doctor ask.

"Yes," Sherri replied, nodding. She turned her head and gave the doctor careful attention, but she also noticed Carter standing off to her side. Sherri was grateful to see Carter, since she had felt so all alone and lost a second before.

"We'll need for you to step over to that desk over there," the doctor told Sherri, pointing. "You'll need to fill out some necessary paperwork, and sign a surgical consent form for us."

"Sure," Sherri agreed, shaking her head more erratically. "Anythang. I jest want my husband taken care of."

"That's what we're here for," the doctor said, trying to add more assurance with a brief smile. "We need to get your husband to the O.R. ASAP," he added. "We'll keep you updated on his progress."

"Thank you, Doctor," Sherri said.

A bob of the doctor's head was his response; then he scurried away to process the next patient. Sherri turned and gave Carter a bittersweet smile. "Guess I need to go over to the desk and kill some time fillin' out paperwork," she said, the tone of her voice relaying the helplessness she felt.

"Yeah," Carter agreed, his head bobbling as he forced a smile of his own. "Hospitals always have plenty of paperwork for ya to fill out. I'm gonna track down Wally's doctor and let him know I need to be kept appraised of his condition. Then I'll go find us a seat in the waitin' room," he said, pointing off to the side with his thumb at the rows of chairs that made up the emergency room waiting area.

"See ya in a bit," Sherri said, turning and making her way over to the desk to fill out whatever essential paperwork was required of her. Sherri knew waiting to hear word on Scott's condition was going to be excruciating, so she did not really mind tying up her time, and her mind, with some written facts for a few moments.

* * * *

When Sherri finished filling out tons of paperwork, she headed for the E.R. waiting room. She spied Carter sitting by a wall, looking up, with a blank expression on his face, at a television mounted on a column in the middle of the room. There was an empty chair beside him with his jacket in it. Sherri guessed that Carter had saved that seat for her. She headed in that direction.

Picking up Carter's jacket and laying it in the next chair down, Sherri sat down in the seat beside Carter. She still had on her long, wool, black coat, and she had no intentions of taking it off, since all she had on underneath was still a halter top and some shorts. Sherri certainly had not had time to change clothes. She had barely had time to grab her winter coat and slip it on.

When Sherri had settled into her chair, Carter looked over at her with remorseful eyes and said, "I'm really sorry about all this, Sherri."

"What in blazes are ya apologizin' for, Carter?" Sherri asked him, sounding a little exasperated.

"You and I both know that Scott should *not* be in that operating room fightin' for his life right now," Carter stated, pointing. "Scott wouldn't have gotten shot if I had done my job the right way," Carter stated with disgust, staring down into his lap.

"Now ya jest wait one cotton pickin' minute, Carter," Sherri chastised. Her eyes had a spark of anger in them now. "I won't have ya downin' yerself; ya hear? We would never have had a chance at catchin' Jeanette if ya hadn't helped us put together the elaborate ploy we did."

"Ya guys would have gotten Jeanette eventually, Sherri, without my help," Carter argued, still sounding dejected and still barely giving her a glance.

"Maybe. But how many people would have had to die before we developed enough of a case against him for prosecution?" Sherri questioned. "It's hard tellin' how many lives we saved by trickin' Jeanette into comin' forward and confessin' to the murders he committed. How much better of a job could ya have done?"

"I should have shot Jeanette when he didn't put his weapons down right away," Carter stated, giving Sherri another apologetic glance.

"Come on, Carter. We're both cops. Ya know as well as I do, that ya jest can't go off and shoot someone like that. Ya've got to give them every opportunity in the world to lay down their weapons. Ya're not God, Carter. Ya couldn't predict that Jeanette would jest…out of the blue…pull the trigger like he did. Ya guys shot as soon as ya could. I don't hold ya responsible for what happened to Scott at all."

"Ya've got a good heart, Sherri," Carter said, reaching to squeeze her hand. There was still a pained grimace on his face. Even though he noticed how pretty Sherri was, Carter had felt funny treating her as a love interest during their sting operation. He actually looked at himself as more of a big brother/father substitute to Sherri. But this image made Carter feel worse about letting Sherri down. "If Scott doesn't pull through, I'll never forgive myself, Sherri."

"Hey…don't talk like that now!" Sherri fussed, pulling her hand away. Her eyes glowed with irritation. "I won't have negative thoughts about Scott. We have to believe that he is goin' to come through this fine. Ya understand?"

"Sure," Carter said, raising and lowering his head a few times. "Sorry," he apologized again.

"Stop apologizin' and feelin' guilty, Carter. Ya aren't helpin' anyone with all this crap. As far as I'm concerned, Scott and I owe ya a debt of gratitude for all ya done for us. Includin'..." she said, drawing closer to him. In a voice just above a whisper, she added, "even loanin' out your bed to us this mornin'."

"I hated that Scott and you had to be parted for so long. He even allowed himself to be placed in jail for a bit..."

"Yeah," Sherri agreed with a bittersweet smile. "When Scott gets involved in somethin', he dun't half-ass it. He allowed himself to be jailed, so he could totally play the part of a suspected serial killer, and jest in case Jeanette came forward and tried to visit him in jail. Scott would have even allowed himself to be tossed in prison if it meant bringin' Jeanette down. I'm jest glad it didn't git to that point."

"Even so...with ya guys bein' practically newlyweds and all, I knew it had to be hell on ya both to be separated like ya was. So givin' ya a place for some private time before everythang came to a head this evenin' was the least I could do," Carter said, fanning his hand out.

"Ya're jest a very carin', intelligent man, Carter," Sherri praised, a friendly grin on her face now. "Ya had all kinds of pressure on ya to solve Jameson Thornton's murder, and Scott was yer prime suspect. Ya could have helped the D.A. build a pretty strong circumstantial case against Scott, but instead, ya chose to pitch in with Scott and me to brang Jeanette forward...and even to git her to confess. Ya're one hell of a cop and an even finer human bein', Carter. So I won't sit here and listen to ya downin' yerself; ya hear?"

"Thanks for your confidence in me and your accolades, Sherri," Carter said, looking down into his lap again. Sherri's comments had not only embarrassed him, but Carter did not think he deserved them. "Any good cop would have done what I done. Ya guys had DNA evidence against Jeanette, so Jeanette needed to come forward. And it was obvious that if Jeanette was tryin' to set Scott up to take the fall for Jameson Thornton's and Joe Butler's murders, then havin' Scott take the fall and broadcastin' a plea for Jeanette to come forward to help with Scott's prosecution was jest a genius plan. And it obviously worked, because Jeanette did come forward."

"Yeah, he did," Sherri agreed, nodding. "And then through yer due diligence, ya found out that one of the stars that Jeanette worked personal security for was none other than Jameson Thornton. That put him up close and personal with Jameson, and gave him opportunity to murder Jameson and set up Scott."

"That weren't too hard to figure out," Carter downplayed, his attention slightly diverted as he watched and listened as a woman in scrubs called out a family name and three individuals got up out of their chairs and followed this woman out of the waiting room. Carter hoped it would not be long before they called out for Sherri and gave her some information on Scott, but he realized it would probably be at least a few hours. He rambled on, "After Jeanette revealed that he was working as a security guard at Dollywood, and further admitted to the fact that this opened him up to opportunities to work as a private security guard to stars, it wa'nt very difficult to do some additional checkin' and find out that one of those stars was Jameson Thornton."

"But if ya wa'nt such a good cop, ya wouldn't have done that checkin'," Sherri continued to argue, a stubborn expression on her face.

Making eye contact with Sherri again, Carter told her, "Given the fact that Wally matched the description of the man dressed as a security guard that appeared at Joe Butler's room right before he was killed, I had to do some addition'l checkin' on Wally's security guard career. And the link I discovered Wally to have to Jameson and Joe, put him very high on my list as our killer. But...it was actually yer doin' that cinched the case fer me. That handwritin' sample ya gave me was a dead match to the handwritin' sample I collected from Wally when I asked for his contact info. Our handwritin' expert confirmed the two samples to be a match, but it was easy enough to see without her expert opinion. I didn't need any more convincin' that Wally was our guy after that."

"But without yer help, Scott and I never could have convinced the D.A. to help with our sting op," Sherri pointed out. "And without the D.A., who had connections with the judge, Scott's attorney, Roland...green thou he was..." she chuckled; then added, "and of course, the media, we couldn't have pulled it all off. Each of these players was essential."

"Rance is a good guy. He wanted to see the right person get punished too. And the right person turned out to be Wally a.k.a. Jeanette. Simple as that."

"Ya're a good guy too, Carter," Sherri assured him, reaching to squeeze his hand. "Let's stop with all the negative and focus on the positive. If Jeanette pulls through, then he is likely going to prison for the rest of his life..."

"Frankly, I hope Jeanette doesn't survive," Carter shared with a low growl, his dark eyes darkening to almost eerie shade of all black.

He noticed a young girl sitting across from him giving him a strange look. She had evidently overheard his hateful remark. Carter regretted he had said these words out loud, even though in his heart, this was exactly how he felt.

"I hope Jeanette *does* survive," Sherri surprised Carter by stating.

"Ya do?" Carter asked, looking away from the young girl's condemning eyes and studying Sherri's instead.

"Yeah. I want to see Jeanette rot away in prison. Death would be the easy way out for this guy," she said.

"I guess ya might have a point there," Carter had to agree. He absentmindedly eyeballed the television again, purposely avoiding making eye contact with any other eavesdropping strangers sitting in the waiting room with them. He had noticed several people had magazines up in front of their faces. People passed the time in all different sorts of ways.

"It'll be okay, Carter," Sherri tried to assure him, giving his hand another squeeze.

"Yeah," he agreed, slowly moving his head up and down as he gave her another glance. *It has to be*, he thought. As the two settled into silence, Carter found himself praying that Scott would come through the surgery alright, and everything would indeed be *okay*.

Chapter 24

Survivors?

Dr. Angela Zemin and her surgical team stood around an operating table, under the brilliant illumination of four rotating operating lamps. They were all covered from head to toe in greenish blue surgical scrubs. Thirty-eight-year old 'Angie', as she liked to be called, had been a successful trauma surgeon for the past five years.

Scott Arnold was the patient on Angie's operating table this evening. Scott was surrounded by machines and had tubes and wires going into his body from all angles. A ventilator helped him breathe; several IV bags of blood replaced what he had lost – and what he was still losing – and a heart monitor carefully kept an eye on his heart rate and blood pressure, both of which were dicey at the moment.

"I need more suction!" Angie barked at the assistant across from her.

This other woman quickly stuck a vacuum hose in the middle of the mushrooming red fluid gurgling up from inside of Scott's abdominal cavity. With a s*woop!*, Scott's abdomen was clear of blood for a moment.

"Clamp!" Angie called and was handed the sterile instrument from another pair of assisting hands. With swift hands, she sealed off a gaping hole in an artery. Scott's blood flow slowed.

Dr. Zemin had been hard at work on Scott's injuries for over two hours. After verifying that the bullet had done no damage to the pancreas, stomach or colon, Angie made the tough decision to remove Scott's spleen. Whenever possible, Angie liked to do a partial splenectomy, because much of the spleen's protective role, such as fighting infections, could be maintained if a small amount of spleen was left behind. But in Scott's case, a partial splenectomy was not an option. The bullet had done too much damage to this organ.

"Sinus rhythm is tacky," Nurse Wilson, a heavyset LPN watching the heart monitor warned. "BP is dropping," she also added.

"Come on, Mr. Arnold, fight with me. We can fix this thing. You have loved ones rooting for you," Angie encouraged as she continued to hurriedly clamp off more bleeders with her adept gloved hands. Angie was known to talk to her patients during surgery. She was a doctor that believed her patients could hear her, and that positive encouragement could help them to survive.

As a piercing alarm pealed from Scott's heart monitor, the grave announcement was made, "He's in V-tach."

"Crash Cart!" Angie called out and swiftly stepped back from the table. She held her blood saturated hands up in the air.

Several other medical aides rushed forward. "Charging," a young doctor by the name of Eric Wheats called out as he held the paddles to a defibrillator over Scott's chest. "Clear," he ordered. Then he pressed the paddles to Scott's chest. Scott's body jerked upward and lowered.

"Still in V-tach," Nurse Wilson announced.

"Push a round of Epi," Angie ordered.

From Scott's other side, a needle was instantly inserted into his IV.

Fresh faced Dr. Wheats, still manning the defibrillator, charged the machine once more with a greater charge.

"Clear," he called again as he pushed the paddles to Scott's chest again.

Scott's body jarred again

"We have sinus rhythm again, but it's still tacky," Nurse Wilson proclaimed.

"Right now, I'll take what I can get," Angie replied, her face cloth moving as she breathed a short sigh of relief. Angie went right back to her task of removing Scott's spleen. "Drop me another liter of blood."

Another bag of blood was hung and attached to one of Scott's IVs.

"Hang in there, Mr. Arnold," Angie half pleaded as she went on frugally working to save this man's life.

* * * *

In the operating room next door, Fifty-five-year-old Dr. Wilson Marks, who had been a surgeon for over fifteen years, and his surgical team, also stood around an illuminated operating table, covered from head to toe in greenish blue surgical scrubs. Their patient was Wallace Cleaver. Like Scott, Wally was also surrounded by machines, which included a heart/BP monitor, and had tubes and wires going into his body from all angles. A ventilator also aided his breathing.

"Doctor, he's seizing again," a nurse called out, as Wally's body began to radically shake and jerk.

"Another round of Dilantin," he quickly prescribed.

One dose of the drug had already been administered an hour before when Wally's body had seized. Another dose was pushed into Wally's IV now. After another few moments of violent shaking, Wally's body settled, but Dr. Marks noted more abnormal posturing. Wally's arms were extended straight and turned toward the body, and his legs were held straight with his toes pointed downward. Dr. Marks realized this posturing could well indicate brain damage. Putting these thoughts aside for now, he continued to probe inside Wally's skull, while another surgeon worked to contain the damage a bullet to Wally's back had done.

* * * *

About an hour later, Dr. Zemin stuck her head into the ER waiting room. "Mrs. Arnold," she called, looking to and fro with big green eyes.

Sherri all but leapt to her feet, glad it was finally her turn for some news. She had watched many individuals vacate their seats and leave the waiting room as their family names were called. Carter arose also and followed closely behind Sherri. He wanted to be nearby whether the news was good or bad.

"I'm Mrs. Arnold," Sherri told the attractive black-haired doctor as she quickly came to stand in front of her. Sherri was jittery as she waited for news.

"Mrs. Arnold, I'm Dr. Angie Zeman," the surgeon briefly introduced herself. "I operated on your husband Scott this evening...."

"H...how is he?" Sherri rushed to ask, not really caring what the doctor's name was. She only wanted the facts of Scott's condition, and she wanted them *now*. The doctor's neutral facial expression gave her no clues.

"Your husband is quite a fighter, Mrs. Arnold. The bullet hit his spleen, which caused massive blood loss. This meant we had to transfuse his blood. He coded on us twice. But he managed to hang in there. He's in our post anesthesia care unit right now. He'll probably be there about another hour or two. Then we plan to move him to ICU for careful observation. But, as of now, he's expected to make a full recovery."

"Oh, thank ya so much, Doctor!" Sherri squealed, fighting not to throw her arms around this woman and give her a big hug and kiss. "When can I see him?" she asked, bouncing on her toes like an excited child.

"ICU is on the fifth floor. If you would like to go on up, there is a waiting room there as well. I'll tell the nurses to call you in the waiting room when Scott has been moved to a room in ICU. Then you can go in to see him. But as I said, he still has another hour or two of observation in PACU first."

"That's fine!" Sherri gushed, so happy she could hardly stand it. She could wait however long it took, now that she knew Scott was going to be alright. It was the waiting and not knowing that had killed her. "I don't know how I can thank you enough, Doctor," she said again.

"I appreciate your gratitude, Mrs. Arnold. But ninety-nine percent of our success rate depends on the patient. And evidently Scott felt he had a reason to stick around, so he fought with us. Somehow I think you might have more than a little something to do with that," she said, giving Sherri a smile.

"Let's hope," Sherri said, giggling.

"I'll be in to check on Scott in the morning. You have a great evening, Mrs. Arnold," the doctor said.

"I will now. Thanks to you," she said, grinning from ear to you.

Dr. Zeman merely returned her smile. Then she turned and headed away.

"That's great news, Sherri," she heard Carter say. Sherri turned and bestowed the tight, happy, relieved hug she had longed to give the doctor on him.

"He's gonna be alright, Carter. Didn't I tell ya?" Sherri said, pulling back from him. Her face was absolutely glowing.

"Yeah, ya did," he said, bouncing his head up and

down. Carter released Sherri from his embrace. "Well, what are we waitin' for? Aren't we goin' up to wait in ICU? I'd like to stick my head in and tell Scott I'm glad he's still around too," Carter told her. He was very relieved and happy as well.

"Let's go. Two hours can't pass quick enough for me," Sherri told him, skipping away toward the elevators.

Carter quickly followed. Once he got Sherri settled in ICU, he fully intended to leave her and go check on the condition of Wallace Cleaver.

* * * *

Carter came back to the ICU waiting room about fifteen minutes after he had left. The expression on his face was somber, matching several of the strangers' faces in the room. There were many others in the room, waiting in recliners. The blankets and pillows in some of the chairs indicated that some of the folks intended to spend the night there waiting on word of a loved one. Carter made his way over to Sherri and plopped down in the chair beside her.

"So what's the verdict?" Sherri asked, extremely curious. Carter had told her, when he left, that he was going to check on Jeanette's condition.

"Well, he's alive," Carter snarled, pinching his lips together. "The bullets did a lot of damage though. His surgeon said Wally – or Jeanette as ya know him – seized twice during surgery, so it's unlikely that he hasn't suffered some significant brain damage. The other bullet lodged in his spine, so Wally more than likely will suffer at least partial paralysis as well."

"Wow!" Sherri commented exhaling. "So I'm guessin' ya think Jeanette's future holds…nursing home instead a jail?"

"That's what I'm thinkin', yeah," Carter agreed, shaking his head with frustration. "If there is substantial brain damage, he probably won't be competent to stand trial. And if he isn't competent to stand trial, then he will walk…"

"Not exactly," Sherri rebutted. "If he's paralyzed he'll probably won't walk," she half teased with dark humor.

"Ha ha," Carter responded, rolling his eyes. "I want that SOB to go to prison where he belongs, Sherri."

"Carter, if Jeanette is truly brain damaged, he'll be in a prison all his own," Sherri argued, feeling little compassion for Jeanette. He had gotten what he deserved in her book. "As long as Jeanette's off the street and not able to kill anymore, I'll be happy," she surprised Carter by saying.

"I guess that's the right way to look at it," he begrudgingly agreed, looking away from Sherri's optimistic eyes.

Carter spied a teenage girl sitting across from him. She had IPOD ear buds stuck in her ears and was munching on Doritos, trying to pass the time. Beside her, an older version of the girl, who Wally guessed to be her mother, wrung her hands and fidgeted in her chair, obviously nervous and restless to hear some word on their loved one.

Carter breathed another sigh of relief that Scott had pulled through and was expected to make a full recovery. But he still believed Wally deserved to pay for having caused Scott pain and suffering and the loss of his spleen. Carter hoped the doctors turned out to be wrong, and Wally had not suffered permanent brain damage. He wanted to see Wally stand trial and go to prison, or receive the death sentence. Carter wanted to see Wally punished to the fullest extent of the law for each and every homicide he committed and for his attempted murder of Scott.

Looking back at Sherri, Carter saw that she had picked up a magazine and was thumbing through the pages. He stared

JUSTICE

up at a television mounted on the wall, watching some comedy.

* * * *

About an hour and a half later, the phone rang in the waiting room for the fifth or sixth time since Carter had been there. Each time the phone rang, a family name was called out by whoever picked up the receiver. People filtered out of the room to go and visit a dear friend or relative that had been moved to his, or her, room in the ICU. This time a man sitting on the other side of the room answered the phone and called out, "Arnold family."

"I'm Mrs. Arnold," Carter heard Sherri say and saw her quickly spring from her chair. She practically bolted across the room and snatched the phone receiver from the stranger's hand. "Yes," Carter heard Sherri say into the receiver. "Thanks!" she chirped. Then she hung up the phone.

When Sherri turned to face Carter again, there was a beaming smile on her face. "Scott has been moved to ICU. He's in room five. Do ya want to go see him?"

"Nah. Ya go ahead. He doesn't need to see my ugly mug. I want him to make a quick recovery, not be scared to death," Carter joked, returning Sherri's smile. "I'll wait until tomorrow, when he's stronger. He needs you now. Ya're the best medicine he can have. In fact…I'm gonna head out," Carter said, standing. He was suddenly finding himself very tired.

He and Sherri walked out into the hall together. Carter pulled the waiting room door closed behind them, "Ya call me if ya guys need anythang," he said.

"Thanks again for everythang, Carter," Sherri said and gave him another brief hug.

The two parted, Carter heading down the stark hallway to the elevators and Sherri swiftly making her way through two large wooden doors and into the ICU. Sherri passed the nurse's station, which was a whirlwind of activity. In fact, two nurses hurried past her as she strolled by some other patients' rooms. Approaching room five, since the walls were made of glass, Sherri could see Scott lying in his bed, hooked up to all kinds of monitoring devices.

Walking into the room and standing at the end of Scott's bed, Sherri stared down at him and thought how small and helpless he looked amongst all the machinery surrounding him. As she listened to the heart monitor's steady *beep, beep, beep* and the *blow/puff* of the oxygen running, a chill ran up Sherri's spine and a lump formed in her throat. The gravity of the fact that she could have so easily lost Scott this evening suddenly settled in on her like a mighty weight. She crept over to the reclining chair beside Scott's bed, took a weary seat, reached out, clutched and rubbed Scott's hand, hung her head, and allowed herself to cry fearful and relieved tears.

A moment later, Sherri felt Scott's hand move. Looking up at his face, she saw that his eyes were open. She sprang out of the chair and bent to bestow a kiss on his forehead. A few stray tears fell and wet Scott's cheeks. When Sherri reached to wipe them away, Scott raised his other arm and grasped Sherri's hand.

"Do I look that bad?" he asked in a garbled, scratchy voice. His throat was extremely sore from the ventilator tube nurses had removed in PACU, and Scott was still very woozy from the anesthetic and the pain medicine they had given him.

"No, sweetheart, yer handsome face is a sight for sore eyes!" Sherri swore, kissing him again, gently on the lips this time, and stroking his cheek. Sherri's eyes filled with tears again, but this time they were tears of joy. "Put yer hand down and relax now, Mr. Arnold," Sherri coaxed. Gently sliding her hand loose from his, she sat back down in her chair and took Scott's closest hand into hers instead. "I'll be right here by yer side. I'm not goin' anywhare. But ya need yer rest now."

"Jeanette?" Scott managed to get out.

"He's here at the hospital too. Both Carter and another cop shot him; one in the back and one in the head. He's alive, but not in the best of shape. But don't ya worry about him for now. We done what we set out to do. We got him off the street," Sherri told Scott, squeezing his hand and giving him a happy smile.

"Then it was all worth it," Scott said, smiling before he laid his head back on the pillow. He fell back into a peaceful sleep; content that they had gotten a murderer off the street and his sweet Sherri was in the room by his side.

Chapter 25

Vegetable

Carter went back to the hospital the next morning. He headed to the ICU to inquire about Wally's condition. Upon presenting his detective's badge to the head nurse, he was told she would page Wally's doctor for him.

Carter only had to wait about ten minutes. Then he was approached by a tall, slim, grey-haired gentleman in a white coat. The name stitched on the man's coat read: Dr. Samuel Peats.

"Hello, Lieutenant," the doctor greeted him. Offering his hand, he told him, "I'm Dr. Peats and I'm Wallace Cleavers' attending physician. What can I help you with?"

"Nice to meet ya, Dr. Peats," Carter continued the pleasantries. Then he got right to the point. "I need to know the condition of suspected serial killer Wallace Cleaver. I was told last night that he might have suffered some brain damage and paralysis. Has he been further evaluated?"

"Yes, he has," the doctor replied, rubbing his lower lip. Before he could continue he was interrupted by a nurse who needed to ask him a question about another patient. "One second," he said to Carter, holding up a finger. Dr. Peats quickly addressed the nurse's issue; then turning his attention back to Carter, he revealed, "Wallace Cleaver's condition *has* been further evaluated, Lieutenant. Upon further testing, we have found that he is totally unresponsive to external stimuli. In other words, he's in a persistent vegetative state."

"So he's a vegetable," Carter grunted, grinding the toe of his shoe into the shiny vinyl floor, as if he were trying to pulverize an invisible cigarette. "Is there any chance of recovery?"

"The chance of recovery is slim to nil," the doctor informed him, crossing his arms, shaking his head, and grimacing. "Some patients sometimes regain a degree of awareness after being in a persistent vegetative state. But the majority remain in this state for years or even decades."

"Crap!" Carter swore under his breath, lowering his head and rubbing his forehead. "Well…I guess it is what it is," he stated, loudly exhaling with annoyance.

"Yes, it is," the doctor agreed, nodding. "Since we can locate no next of kin, Wallace Cleaver will likely be moved to our skilled nursing facility next door after his recovery. That's where he will likely spend the rest of his days."

"Okay. Thanks for sharing his prognosis with me, Doc," Carter said.

"Sure thing," the doctor said. Another nurse walked up and demanded the doctor's attention. So Carter sunk his hands into his pant's pockets and slowly moved away. As he turned, Carter caught sight of Sherri coming from Scott's ICU room.

Sherri smiled when she saw Carter and approached him. "Did ya come to see Scott?" she asked.

"Ya betcha," Carter said, trying to sound upbeat, even though Wally's grim diagnosis still weighed heavily upon his mind.

"Come on. I'll take ya in," Sherri said, turning and heading back toward Scott's room.

Carter followed at her heel, happy for the brief diversion.

* * * *

Louise Samuels, an elderly neighbor of Wally's, had been babysitting Susanna. Since Wally had no family, he had made friends with this caring lady that lived across the street from him. Wally had even gone so far as to list Louise as his emergency contact, so the hospital had called her when he had been admitted the evening before. Louise had kept Susanna all night and had taken her to preschool the next morning.

When Louise came to pick Susanna up from preschool that afternoon, she was met by a Sevier County Social Services' representation, who presented a warrant to take Susanna into their custody.

"What will happen to the child?" Louise asked, fearful for Susanna. She thought the little girl was darling and hated to see her shuffled from foster home to foster home. Louise had heard horror stories about foster care.

"She'll be placed with a foster family as soon as we find a suitable home environment for her," the young woman from social services rattled off to Louise, seeming emotionless.

Susanna was still in a classroom, sitting at a table coloring. The adults were out in the hallway talking. They had already had several parents pass them by, going into the classroom to pick up their child.

"Can't I just take her in?" Louise asked, her heart and not her head talking. Louise was seventy-two years old. Her hunched back was a clear sign of the osteoporosis she already suffered, and she had a multitude of other age-related health problems as well.

"If you would like to sign up to be a foster parent, you might be considered," the social service worker told her, even though she knew it was unlikely Louise would be chosen to be a foster parent. "But for now, I need to take Susanna with me," the woman told both Louise and Susanna's preschool teacher.

"I'll go git her for you," the preschool teacher, a young, dark-haired, twenty-something lady, said, with a heavy heart. She hated to see Susanna go into Social Services as well. But she realized there was nothing she could do to prevent this awful thing from transpiring.

Susanna's teacher opened the door to the classroom and made her way over to Susanna. She took Susanna by the hand and led her out into the hallway. "Susanna, this is Ms. Kitterling," she told the little girl with a pasted on smile. "She's going to take you where there are other little boys and girls for you to play with."

Susanna looked from the lanky, young, blond-haired, social services' worker to her white-haired, wrinkled, bent-over friend, Louise. "I go with Louise," Susanna said, pointing and smiling. She also began making her way to this much older lady, who she trusted.

"No," Susanna's preschool teacher protested, even though she did not want to. "Susanna, you need to go with Ms. Kitterling for now."

"Susanna," Louise said, cradling the child's small, adorable, innocent face with her garbled arthritic hands. Louise's voice was shaky and she held back tears. "Ya'll have all sorts of fun with Ms. Kitterling. Ya'll git ta color and play all sorts of games. It'll be rally fun," she lied.

"Where's my daddy?" the perceptive child asked.

"Daddy's in the hospital right now, Susanna. Ms. Kitterling is going to watch over you until daddy gits better," Louise fabricated again, releasing the girl's face.

Susanna turned and studied the blond-haired lady with her big, curious, brown eyes. Ms. Kitterling stuck her hand out, "Come on, Susanna. Come with me. It's where your daddy wants for you to be right now," this stranger told her in a cheery, high-pitched voice.

Susanna looked past Ms. Kitterling to her preschool teacher. When she saw her teacher smile and nod, Susanna reluctantly reached out and linked her hand to the blond-haired stranger's.

Ms. Kitterling wasted no time leading the little girl toward the front door and her outside awaiting car. Susanna's preschool teacher and Louise watched with dejected eyes as Susanna disappeared out the front door with the social worker. Both of their hearts were breaking for Susanna, but they knew deep down that there was nothing they could do. Susanna was now a ward of the state.

* * * *

Scott was released from the hospital five days later. A few days after that, Wally was moved from the hospital into the long-term, skilled care facility within Fort Sanders Sevier Medical Center. The D.A. was no longer interested in trying to pursue criminal charges against Wally, since he was certainly not competent to stand trial.

When news broke of the elaborate scheme that Carter, the D.A., Sherri and Scott had hatched to capture the *real* serial killer in their area, the story became a media magnet. Rance Dooley was suddenly thrust full force into the public eye, with popular shows such as Dateline and Oprah vying for him to appear to tell his story of his brilliant ruse. Carter, Scott and Sherri were also approached for their input, but they declined to comment, wanting to fade back into the woodwork.

* * * *

About a month after Wally had been moved to Fort Sanders Sevier Nursing Home, Scott paid him an unexpected visit. He found Wally sitting hunched over in a wheelchair in the community room, amongst several other men and woman that sat in, or were strapped into, wheelchairs. The patients that were bedridden had to be gotten out of bed each day to prevent them from getting bedsores.

Wally had a ball cap on his head. This cap was there to cover up the grotesque gully that the bullet blast had left in the top of his skull. But regardless of the camouflage, if Wally's head was raised, a sizable indention was visible in his forehead.

The nursing home smelled like a combination of urine, feces and Clorox. The dedicated staff did what they could to keep the facility smelling fresh, but it was a never-ending task with so many of their residents consistently soiling themselves.

Scott grabbed the handles of Wally's wheelchair and wheeled him over in front of a window, where the sun was shining on his face. "The sun feels good, doesn't it, *Jeanette?*" Scott asked him.

Wally just continued to hang his head, no sign of recognition of anything Scott had said. He stared with glassy, wide eyes down into his lap, and drool occasionally dripped from his bottom lip.

"I just came to visit you today in hopes that some part of you can still hear me," Scott told him, glancing up from Wally's distorted body and out the window at the brown grass and bare trees of February. "You see, Jeanette, you may not be going to prison for what you did, but you are stuck in this nursing home in a body that won't work anymore. So you are stuck in your own private, hellish prison. And that suits me just fine. Justice has still been served, my friend," Scott sarcastically growled, as he bent to a stoop. "Oh, and one other thing you should know," he said and smiled. "Sherri and I are raising Susanna now. She talked me into signing up as foster parents so we can take her in. So you won't get your chance at ruining her life either. Just thought you should know all that.

As I said, I sure hope some part of you can still process this information," he said. Standing, Scott added, "You have a great life, Jeanette."

Walking away, Scott left Jeanette's wheelchair by the window. In the doorway of the community room, Scott stopped, and turned, taking one final glance at Jeanette. Jeanette was still pathetically hanging over in his chair. Scott had no idea whether Jeanette had heard, or more specifically comprehended, anything he had said. But it had given Scott a great deal of satisfaction to be able to see Jeanette in such miserable shape and to tell him what he had. Scott realized, if any part of Jeanette was able to discern what he had said, it would eat away at Jeanette. Scott only hoped he could be so lucky.

For Debbie, all the other helpless victims you killed, and their families, you worm, Scott thought with contempt as he headed for the exit door, never to return.

Chapter 26

The Wink

Winter gave way to a beautiful temperate spring, and spring gave way to a hot and arid summer as Wally passed five more months at Fort Sanders Sevier Nursing Home.

One day, midmorning, a commotion arose as one of the nurses, a plump woman by the name of Sheila Parks, went to check on a resident by the name of George Wilson. A moment later, Sheila dashed out of the room, yelling to Barbara, the clerk at the nurse's station, "Call an ambulance. George isn't breathing!"

Wally was sitting in his wheelchair, in the hall by the nurse's station, staring blankly into space. As another nurse and several aides ran by, scurrying to George's room to see what they could do to help, a breeze fanned Wally. George Wilson was a sixty-nine-year-old African American, who was the picture of health, other than some dementia, which kept him from living alone.

Since the hospital was right next door to the nursing home, it only took five minutes for a siren's wail to be heard in the parking lot. Two paramedics entered the building and charged past Wally's and other patients' wheelchairs, and around residents standing and walking in the hall. They stormed into George Wilson's room.

Moments later, one by one, the nurses, aides, and paramedics all came out of George's room with saddened and troubled expressions on their faces. "Call the coroner," Sheila instructed Barbara with a hard scowl on her face as she approached the desk.

"You mean...George died?" Barbara asked in shock, her greenish blue eyes perplexed. "What happened?"

"We don't know for sure. The paramedics said they think maybe a heart attack. We won't know for certain until the county medical examiner makes his determination," Sheila told her.

"Man...I can't believe this. George was so healthy," Barbara commented to Sheila and to herself. She picked up the phone to call the coroner and have him come and pick up George Wilson's body.

As Sheila, the head nurse, passed by Wally, one eye moved, appearing to wink at her.

"Sheila," the clerk called out to her, pulling the receiver away from her ear.

"Huh?" Sheila replied, stopping and turning her head in Barbara's direction.

"It looked like Mr. Vegetable there just winked at you," Barbara told Sheila, pointing.

"First off, Barbara," Sheila said, her tone stern and her hands on her hips. "The patient's name is Wallace Cleaver. Wally for short. He's not Mr. Vegetable," she chastised, a spark of annoyance in her eyes.

"Sorry," Barbara apologized. "I didn't mean anything really," she tried to excuse, her eyes contrite. "I was just shocked to see him wink; that's all."

Sheila stepped back over to Wally. He was staring straight ahead again with no sign of responsiveness. "It was probably a spontaneous movement; that's all," Sheila commented. "That sometimes happens with folks in a vegetative state," she shared her knowledge. "Did you call the coroner?" she asked, changing the subject.

"Not yet. I was on the phone when I...when I thought he winked," Barbara explained, placing the receiver to her ear again.

Sheila turned and hurried away down the hall. There were a lot of residents in the hallways that were upset, and it was her and the aides job to settle them all down.

When Wally was certain no one was looking, he lowered his head and allowed himself to shake with silent, yet deep, laughter.

The End

Continue the journey….

You have just completed *Sissy Marlyn's* eighth novel. Thank you so much for reading!

There will be more novels coming for you to lose yourself in from *Sissy Marlyn*. Still planned for 2008:

Bluegrass
(Third novel in the "B" Women's Fiction Series)

Check out:

www.sissymarlyn.com
www.bearheadpublishing.com/sissy.html

For updates on new novels being written and appearances.

Thank you!

Sissy Marlyn

CPSIA information can be obtained at www.ICGtesting.com
Printed in the USA
LVOW06s1200010614

388016LV00001B/89/P